I0572183

# Girl from the North Country

William Lynch

Cabbage Creek Press
Ponte Vedra Beach, Florida

Book Design by Sagaponack Books & Design
Map of Scotland from the National Library of Scotland
Photograph of the author by Amy Cornett Photography
Cover photograph of Kilchurn Castle from Library of Congress

ISBN 978-1-7331026-0-5 (softcover)
ISBN 978-1-7331026-1-2 (hardcover)
ISBN 978-1-7331026-2-9 (e-book)

Library of Congress Catalog Card Number: 2019905663

Summary: Late nineteenth century historical fiction about western Scotland and characters who lived, loved, and died there.

FIC014000 Fiction / Historical / General
FIC051000 Fiction / Cultural Heritage
FIC027160 Fiction / Romance / Historical / Scottish

Cabbage Creek Press
Ponte Vedra Beach, Florida

First Edition

This book is dedicated to Jacob, Colin, and Hailey.

# 1850s Western Scotland

# Contents

# The Bully Boy of Ayrshire

*T*he thing Duncan Keillor remembered most was not the shame of seeing his father Graeme stagger drunkenly out of the Blair Mine manager's office, having been fired for the fourth time in Duncan's young memory. Rather, his mind's eye saw tears roll down the cheeks of his sainted mother Annag, after Duncan practically carried his father home and told her the sorry story of Graeme having appeared at the mine drunk and unable to work safely. He had consumed a prodigious amount of homemade pot still whisky from who knows where. The tears were Annag's recognition that they would again be forced to move lodgings for their family of five and start over, with no wages and cold and hunger in the interim.

Graeme's own mum and dad had struggled with alcohol and had succumbed to liver disease or related maladies. Along with many others from similar situations, Graeme, when only a young boy, was quickly displaced to the Waifs and Strays Society run by the Roman Catholic Church. The orphanage proved a desperate place with too little food, clothing, or warmth; it offered nothing to nurture children, apart from a roof to shield them from the cold wind and rain sweeping off the Irish Sea and across Scotland. The nuns, who wore white, heavily starched, formal cornettes and habits over their black tunics, kept some semblance of order with threats of reduced rations or beatings or sometimes both. The constant terror and depravation had a dreadful impact on the psyches of these poor children, which followed them into their lives and the lives of their families.

The bleak orphanage had acquired an informal nickname, "Foundlings," which inferred the children housed there had been abandoned by their parents rather than orphaned by their deaths. This negative connotation further demonized these children, some not much older than infants. Despite the mostly noble intentions of the nuns, a culture of stronger over weaker naturally developed among the older children, with bullying, threats, menacing, and intimidation of those who were younger and vulnerable. The lucky ones had older siblings or friends who looked out for them as protectors.

Graeme, not so fortunate, suffered innumerable beatings at the hands of these toughs, grunting and moaning from the blows and kicks, but never once shedding a tear. He learned the best course of action to be no response when the nuns asked him about the source of his bruises, contusions, and scrapes. In time, these cruel ruffians found others to torment. Graeme survived and when he was turned out by the orphanage on his twelfth birthday—undernourished and psychologically damaged—he knew he had only himself and his wits to depend on.

In those times, youngsters living out on the streets was not an uncommon thing. These urchins survived by sleeping in doorways or stables, or anyplace out of the wet and the cold. They were like some type of feral animal whose needs were minimally satisfied, never having a whole meal. They subsisted on bread crusts, scraps, or mostly spoiled food, getting what meager sustenance they could from garbage bins or filched items from homes or grocers. They worked jobs which no one else took on: mopping floors in pubs, cleaning out backhouses, mucking stables, hauling coal from bins to stoves, often all the while stealing food or clothing at the real risk of hellish beatings. The scars from such efforts were vivid, but mostly internal and invisible. For them to survive into their teenage years took inner strength and cunning, and caused either distrust in others or total detachment from life. A thick skin developed along with cold-bloodedness in the eyes. The idea of a kindness being given or received remained outside the understanding of these young people. The odds for any semblance of a good life were stacked against Graeme and those like him.

He provided for himself as the years went by. Among others cast into destitution, his expectations were lowered considerably. Having a warm, dry place to sleep and meals at regular intervals he deemed as living successfully. Mind-numbing and often dangerous work became the rule for these lost souls as they aged into young adults, with few thinking beyond the next several days or weeks. They existed in an environment unlikely for positive development or good behavior, and life was something to be endured while their psyches hardened.

In time, Graeme Keillor found himself, in his late teens, working in the iron and coal mines around Ayrshire, Scotland, in the worst of jobs, normally as a pumper at the bottom of the mine. Despite a slight physique, his muscles were hard. His mop of ginger-hued hair topped a continuously flushed face as he toiled at the hand pump. Often alone for hours and hours, he ended the day exhausted and dreaded the next. He had a reputation as a hard worker with a thirst for any kind of alcoholic beverage he could manage to buy on his paltry wage. For most men, pumper was a starter job to get you established in the mine until you had proven yourself worthy of a chance at a position requiring a basic skill or at least one necessitating an elemental level of thinking. Mornings, Graeme began weakened by the effects of whatever alcoholic potion he had consumed the night before to dull his rage at his lot in life. This continued condition placed him in a situation of being deemed unworthy for anything other than the most mindless, physically demanding, wretched jobs the mine could offer, surely viewed as nothing more than a death spiral.

Graeme's work ethic, born of necessity, allowed him to maintain a continuity of work early on, staying in the same places often for months at a time. While nearly devoid of social skills, he spent his nights at the pub wrapping his thick, scarred hands around a large mug of stout. His demeanor then took on a different persona and his body visibly relaxed as though the alcohol worked some type of magic on his psyche. He began to quietly converse with others around him, mostly listening, sometimes participating in a discussion about simple things, like the weather. It is a stretch to say he developed friendships; at least, others considered him a part of their social fabric. Mostly they were young men like him, often with families. They began to disperse after an hour or two, while Graeme continued to work himself into a level of inebriation such as to render himself almost nonfunctional. He staggered to his shabby room, falling into bed and a deep sleep. Miraculously, he seldom missed work or arrived late, as if some inner sense of self-preservation roused him at the proper time. The woman who rented him the room saw to it that his meal bucket had some bread and tea in it each morning. While he got by, the daily experience was marginal at best.

Nearing twenty, he worshipped alcohol. Filled with as many hormones as the next man, he was not above succumbing to natural urges, normally involving an ugly trollop met in or outside whatever public house he frequented at the time. There was nothing loving or tender in these assignations, only quick, rushed, almost violent sex filled with grunts and heavy breathing instead of whispers and moans. In his desperate existence as a man of his station and circumstance, he simply could not expect to be deemed attractive to a comely lassie of any repute at all. And then he chanced to meet Annag McShanog.

Annag, eighteen and plain, with a round face, ruddy cheeks, and sandy red hair cropped off at her shoulders, was thin and poorly dressed in a drab servant's uniform—silent indications that she had struggled with life as much as Graeme. Annag's parents had both perished tragically in a tenement fire when she was only eight. A kindly aunt in her late fifties, widowed and childless, took her in as her own, sparing her from the tragedy of life in an orphanage. The aunt's name, Jesse McShanog, worked as a chambermaid for a reasonably prosperous family in Kilmarnock; she had recently cut back her workload due to her age. Annag and Jesse needed each other now and their life together was truly a blessing.

Jesse did the best for Annag that she could. They shared a warm, dry room on the ground floor of a building next door to a hotel in the center of town, a safe area. Annag helped Jesse in her work for the Stewart family, and they shared meals in the spotless kitchen of the fine home.

After work, they walked the several blocks to their lodgings and, some days, stopped in at the Catholic school on the way. Annag sat, listening intently, in the back of a room where a nun taught letters and numbers to girls about her age—not exactly a formal education, yet a chance for some rudimentary instruction. They led a tranquil life and developed much affection for each other; they were partners in a quest for survival during an unforgiving time in a mostly impoverished area.

On Sundays, they sat in a pew and worshiped at the back of the church's sanctuary while the priest intoned a homily in Latin. Almost none of the congregation understood a word of it; they nodded obediently rather than admit their ignorance and lack of understanding. Annag's parents had been practicing members of the Church of Scotland. Annag understood not much of the meaning of Presbyterianism, or Catholicism either, for that matter. The church was close by and this weekly outing was much enjoyed and anticipated—a break from the humdrum of daily life. The choice of a denomination and the fundamentals of a faith were not something they dwelled on.

Jesse regularly fed them healthy food and kept them clean and warm. There was no room for much luxury of any type, save for the Christmas pudding they enjoyed each year at the Stewarts'. And sometimes the family also provided warm clothing, previously worn by the older Stewart children, which were well made and practical, as opposed to fashionable. Annag was thankful and felt no shame in the enjoyment of another's castoffs. Annag and Jesse had a happy time for a while.

When Annag became fifteen, she noticed a change come over Jesse. It was not sudden, but more gradual, with the obvious loss of weight and a slowness to her walk, coupled with a dull gray complexion. Jesse shrugged it off as normal aging, while Annag worried, as did the Stewarts' head cook, who prevailed on Mrs. Stewart to have a doctor come and examine Jesse. The physician shook his head after examining her and told Jesse he feared she had a malignancy—a death sentence in those times.

Jesse's only worry was the care and well-being of Annag. She begged the Stewarts to look after her when she couldn't. This was highly unusual in rural Scotland, where a maintained differentiation of the social classes existed. Bridget Stewart, a true Christian woman, promised Jesse to find a good situation for Annag. This brought great peace of mind to Jesse, and she passed away within a few weeks. Annag felt orphaned once again.

Bridget reached out to her husband's cousin, a prosperous merchant in Ayrshire. After much back and forth, they agreed that Annag would become part of the servant staff at the cousin's country home near Dalry, North Ayrshire. Annag was untrained, and only a pittance of compensation was available in addition to room, board, and a uniform allowance. Nevertheless, she was warm and safe and able to make a life for herself. Annag was mistrusted by the existing staff, who were jealous that she had a connection, however distant, to the owners. Over time, Annag settled into at least a modicum of belonging, and things quieted down.

The work was not hard, yet was mind-numbing in its repetition: constant cleaning and polishing, sweeping and washing, carrying in coal, and taking out chamber pots. The Stewarts did not visit often, never more than twice a month. Despite this, the visits caused frenetic preparation to ensure the family remained pleased with the servant staff's work, thus securing their employment. Having a second home in the country was more of a status symbol than a practicality, and James Stewart was keen on status. Bridget tried to make sure Annag fit in and asked after her well-being, much to the dismay of the other jealous members of the staff. For a teenaged orphan in the hardscrabble Scottish countryside, Annag did well as the months and years passed.

Saturdays, with the family not in residence, Annag walked the kilometer or so into Dalry on errands for the head housekeeper and to enjoy some fun on her own. Sometimes, late in the afternoon, she stopped in at a pub called The Old Speckled Hen and enjoyed a glass of Tennent's lager. She didn't much care for the taste of the alcohol, yet appreciated the chance for some exposure to other young people who smiled and laughed and were friendly to her. Scarcely able to afford the tuppence for the weak lager, she sat and nursed it, eagerly listening to the others chat about their lives. They discussed work, weather, food, parents, children, relationships, sometimes hinting as to their sexual prowess. Annag was inexperienced in joys of the heart. Not a prude, she looked forward to these social opportunities and, over time, became part of the group, even talking and laughing occasionally. Careful to return to the Stewarts' before nightfall, she walked back to the village the next morning for services at the local Church of Scotland, taking after the denomination of her long-dead parents.

Things went on like this for quite some time. Late one cold Saturday afternoon, she joined her friends after walking in a light snow to get to the pub. She had shaken off her coat and sat down on a stool, when a drunken ruffian staggered up to her and placed his arms around her in a tight embrace.

"You'll be giving me that wet kiss now, lass!"

Shocked, Annag started to cry in protest, when she heard a bellow: "Get your damned paws off her!"

The ruffian, embarrassed at being taken to task for his loutish behavior, drew back his fist. She saw a strong man, a bit older than her, grab the ruffian's fist in his calloused hand, twisting it behind the young man's back, while his other hand grabbed the lout's collar. He thrust him out the door of the pub, into the snow. The bartender came from behind the bar and told the man out in the snow to stay away from his pub. Annag's friends cheered loudly and clapped the strong man on the back. He nodded to Annag and walked to the back of the bar.

"Hooray for old Graeme Keillor!" said one of her friends.

"Graeme who?" a flustered Annag shouted to her friend, Rona.

Rona replied that Graeme, a miner, often came to the pub and normally kept to himself.

Rona whispered to Annag, "He has been quietly watching you for several weeks now, trying to muster the courage to speak to you. The drunk putting his hands on you sent him over the edge. You have an admirer and protector."

Annag blushed and kept to herself until time to leave. She put on her damp coat and walked to the back of the bar where Graeme sat by himself, nursing a mug of stout. Her face turned crimson when she held out her hand and thanked him for defending her from the unwelcome advances of the lout. With a shy smile, he gave a nod of his head.

As she turned to leave, he asked, "Will you do me the honor of having a meal with me next Saturday?"

Unable to speak, Annag quickly nodded and dashed out of the pub, into the snowy evening. Halfway back to the Stewarts', she realized she didn't know the time for the meeting next Saturday with Graeme. She shook her head and figured to appear there as normal and see if things worked out.

The week passed very slowly for Annag. She had trouble focusing; her mind could barely handle the excitement she felt about the upcoming rendezvous with Graeme Keillor. She didn't mention it to any of her co-workers, fearful of what the head housekeeper might do or say. Annag decided to wear the simple dark blue dress she normally wore to church services. While it might have been too formal for a meal in a pub, it was all she really had, save her chambermaid's uniform and some worn and torn casual attire.

On Saturday, she used a cloth to wash her body, dried off, and put on the blue dress. She pulled on her coat and walked into the chill afternoon, purposefully striding into the village. It was late afternoon when she wandered into The Old Speckled Hen and took an open seat at a table.

After a moment, she looked to see Graeme shyly walking to the table to join her. His face appeared freshly washed and his hair combed; he wore clean work clothes. With one of his large hands wrapped around a half-empty pint of stout, he sat down. They began to chat, both feeling awkward yet seemingly happy. Annag enjoyed a glass of lager while Graeme nursed a second stout. They had what today we call a classic pub meal: a meat pie with a crust which covered a mixture of mutton, carrots, turnips, and mashed potatoes. They ate slowly, adding bits of salt and pepper, savoring the taste and texture of the common meal. They were oblivious to the noisy goings-on around them in the tavern. They both relaxed and enjoyed the late-afternoon nourishment.

After the meal, Annag stood and put on her coat, thanking Graeme for the fine time. He rose and took her elbow, proud to accompany her home. And so they walked the long way back to the Stewarts'. Saying good night, Annag gave him a peck on the cheek and quickly went into the darkened house. Graeme slowly walked into the gloaming, back to the pub in town.

Things went on between them for some time, meeting almost every week. Occasionally they took a walk through the town, chatting about whatever came into their minds. One afternoon, Graeme guided them on a different route, into an area on the edge of the village. The buildings, while not exactly run-down, were well-worn and fading. The couple turned down an alley and, around the back, a set of wooden stairs led to a two-room apartment.

Graeme pulled a key from his pants pocket and opened the door. The rooms were barren except for a small square table and two wooden chairs, a faded mattress on a metal bedspring, and a dresser with three open drawers. A closet-like alcove with a cloth drape over the opening was tucked near a corner. Each room had a glass window covered by tattered curtains. The sink had no running water and a coal stove provided both heat and a cooking surface.

"What do you think?" he asked shyly, almost talking to his shoes.

"I thought you had a place close to the mine," a puzzled Annag responded.

Looking into her eyes, Graeme said, "I mean the place to be for us."

Annag began to sob, and he took her into his arms, kissing her on the lips.

Despite the clumsy proposal, Annag was swept off her feet and overcome with the most joy she had ever experienced in her young life.

Two weeks later, they married. Following the simple ceremony, Mrs. Stewart had insisted on hosting a light lunch in her home, which Annag found awkward since they were served by her co-workers. Graeme was well behaved and appreciated the hard cider provided as their beverage. Afterwards, the newlyweds walked from the luncheon, back to their apartment in the village.

It might be unfair to say they were prepared for consummating their marriage. Annag had never been with a man and her only knowledge of lovemaking came from the coarse talk she had listened to from her friends at the bar and infrequent whispers from her fellow servants. She, extremely nervous, had no self-confidence, fearing to be deemed unworthy by her husband. Graeme, who had never had sex where any type of love or gentle tenderness had been involved, figured he could manage. Their first sex act was quick and painful for her; still, Graeme's love for Annag made it a passionate experience. They did not have the luxury of lingering because the next morning, Graeme was off early to the mine and Annag later walked to the Stewart residence.

Since a large portion of Annag's compensation consisted of the Stewarts' room and board, an accommodation had to be made for her labor. They increased the coinage paid every fortnight and allowed her to take home food as well as continue to provide her breakfast and lunch. Graeme and Annag did their best to establish a household and respect one another's needs and independence.

Things went well for quite some time, and then one night Graeme didn't come home from work as expected. Annag went to bed worried, while not deeply fearing his absence. Very late, she heard him staggering up the stairs, drunk from an evening grog stop which he had lost control of. She was both relieved and angry, and told him so. The slap of his hand across her face—quick, hard, and painful—was followed by forced sex devoid of love or tenderness. Annag's spirits were crushed. She tried to rationalize her husband's behavior as a mistake fueled by alcohol.

He had gone to work when she awoke. She forced herself to report to work at the Stewarts', unable to hide her bruised face. The other servants tittered and pointed, whispering to one another. Annag's shame was almost unbearable. Fortunately, she thought, the owners were not in residence at the time.

That evening when Graeme came home sober, he saw the bruises and looked away. He didn't apologize and in fact didn't see a need to, reasoning that his actions had been the normal behavior he had seen and experienced his whole life. And so the abuse became a pattern, and Annag felt guilty, always working harder to please her husband and demonstrate her worthiness.

Alcohol consumption and the resulting drunkenness became more and more a central point of Graeme Keillor's life. One Saturday he staggered home early, hopelessly muckered. He had been caught going to a pub on his lunch break—a serious breach of mine rules—and had been discharged by the superintendent. He promptly went back to the pub and wasted more of the money they were counting on to make the rent. Another miner brought him home and told Annag of a mine some twenty miles away that was desperate for workers. She wept with the knowledge of being forced to move and having to abandon her arrangement at the Stewarts'.

They stayed in the next day and, on Monday Graeme walked to the new mine, hoping to find work and promising to send word to Annag.

She told the head housekeeper of her misfortune and, surprisingly, didn't receive much understanding or accommodation.

She was paid for the work she had already performed and was promised a referral should she need one. The woman wanted Annag to turn in her uniform. She had no other clothing with her; she had been hopeful she could continue working until she had word from Graeme. The others avoided her. Annag took off the uniform, putting on her coat over her undergarments.

She cried softly as she walked, shivering in the light snow, back to the apartment in the village. The landlord was there and demanded the rent. He took the few coins she had received as payment until the end of the week. She had no food and no coal for warmth, and the next day she began to pack their meager belongings.

They struggled in the new town. Graeme's wage was the same, but the supplement Annag scrambled to bring in from part-time work as a random chambermaid fell far short of what they were used to. Their single room was shabby, and the desultory existence dispirited Annag. She pressed on. The cycle continued, with Graeme's drunkenness eventually leading to a firing at whatever mine he had managed to find work. The potential of life together meant a sudden relocation and constantly running from his reputation. While there were some brief periods of quasi-stability, in the end Graeme relapsed and they were forced to move on.

Eventually, Annag found herself pregnant, terrified at the thought of bringing a newborn child into a world she had no control over. They were barely making ends meet. Graeme straightened his behavior for a while, and Annag had an uneventful pregnancy. A family she had worked for arranged elementary medical care through a midwife. After a long labor, a healthy baby boy was born, whom they named Duncan. Moved by fatherhood, Graeme worked extra hours at the mine to compensate for the loss of Annag's income. Annag, happier than she had been for some time, started to feel hopeful about their family and her prospects.

With the birth of Duncan, the physical abuse had stopped. After a time, though, the frequent drunkenness returned. The cycle continued over some years, with numerous mine jobs, subsequent firings, and moves to dreary lodgings. Duncan bore the brunt of the continued itinerancy, constantly being the new kid in town. He was resentful and embarrassed by his father's behavior.

When he was younger, some older boys yelled "Son of the drunk" at him in a teasing manner, until he broke down emotionally and tried to fight them—which had all along been their intention. They encircled him, each one getting in a few punches before knocking him down. Then they kicked or piddled on him until the humiliation was complete. Afterwards, they laughed and moved on, trying to find another "mollycoddle" to punish. Duncan developed an unhealthy, destructive, internal rage at these injustices, demons which challenged him throughout much of his life.

Fighting developed as a learned behavior for Duncan Keillor. In time, he became the boy with a continual perceived grudge to settle, which put him in a position to be the older, stronger, and more confident one. It became sport to make the younger ones cry or subject them to punches and kicks for no reason. Other toughs looked at him in admiration, reinforcing his antisocial behavior and causing Duncan to relish inflicting pain and suffering. Careful in choosing his victims, he made sure there was no protector to be dealt with. He specialized in having the first punch come without warning, its ferocity overwhelming and effective, followed by kicks until the victim fell, broken and weeping. Then some name-calling inflicted additional emotional damage on the victims as the fury of the assaults took hold of Duncan. He was able to keep knowledge of this behavior away from Annag because they moved so often; she had no idea of her son's violent reputation.

Duncan was barely twelve years old the day his father was fired, in 1856, by the Blair Coal Mine near Dalry, well south of Glasgow in Ayrshire, on Scotland's west coast. Now the eldest of three children, Duncan had not only to look out for himself, but also his two sisters, Brighid and Moira. Graeme and Annag moved the family like nomads, wandering the countryside looking for work and accommodations they could afford. They were always one step ahead of Graeme's reputation. It was a wonder Annag kept her sanity; she was always in fear of not having the basic needs for her family. Graeme quickly evolved from a pitiful drunk into a hopeless alcoholic. Shame had a powerful effect on the developing personalities of his children. While Duncan was a boastful bully able to maintain a social standing, his sisters were veritable ragamuffins, always with downcast glances and never speaking directly to anyone other than their mother. While Duncan was their protector, a void existed when it came to providing much of a sense of well-being. Annag constantly tried to find the odd job, resorting to begging, if need be. Were it not for the grace of the church, they may well have starved.

And then one evening Graeme did not return from the mine. Annag sent Duncan to see if he had been injured. The mine superintendent said Graeme had left with the others when the shift ended, like any other normal day. Duncan made the rounds of the various public houses, looking for his father. Graeme was well known in the pubs, which fortunately never extended credit for those who frequently were short of the monies for a pint. Then Duncan began to roam the back alleys where some poor souls hid out in groups in coal bins, sharing from communal jugs of illicit poteen, trying to attain or maintain a chosen level of inebriation. Seldom were these fellows workers; rather, they were sots on the way to an untimely demise. Everywhere Duncan went, his father was well known but not to be found.

After several hours, Duncan went home to his mother, and they realized Graeme had walked out on them. Unfortunately, this was not an unknown occurrence among those of their social class. Men walked off, never to be seen or heard from again, leaving their families to certain destitution and suffering.

Annag never spoke of Graeme to her young children again. She was able to get word to Bridget Stewart, who could not provide for them at that time. However, she had a sister, Fiona, who lived in the north with her woolen merchant husband, Ian Steel. Fiona needed a servant for her house staff in Paisley. Besides the work,

Fiona could also provide a kind of lodging above the stables in the back of their home in the city. This was the only chance for Annag and the children and they took it.

They walked and cadged rides on wagons, arriving in three days, cold, hungry, and exhausted. Fiona gave them a keen and experienced once-over, and then she had a servant show them where to sleep. They had no heat or water, save the warmth which drifted upwards from the beasts of burden stabled below; at least they were dry and under a roof. Annag functioned as a chambermaid for the Steels, while Duncan served as a stable boy. The girls stayed out of the way, fretting and wringing their hands over not being able to contribute. They all told themselves it was temporary, and it was, sort of. After a few weeks, a pantry room in the main house was made available, and the four of them moved into the room. The situation provided heat and access to clean water and warm food.

The whole process aged Annag, who carried the burden without rancor. After all, she had not had much luck in her life. She carried on, trying to do the best for her family.

In a few months, they received word that Graeme had been killed in a fight near the port town of Ardrossan. The details were sketchy. He had been working as a laborer at a dock where coal was loaded for shipment on the water. It wasn't clear if the fight took place at the work location or somewhere else nearby; it didn't matter. The authorities had investigated, but no one had been charged. An argument which had gotten out of hand had been settled with a club. His remains were taken to a charity burial place, with no marker or other means of identifying his last resting place—although he had not rested in recent memory, so to speak.

Annag thought it best not to tell the girls and trusted Duncan not to speak of it. Strangely, Duncan did not feel anger towards his father; rather, he felt emptiness and a void which he didn't understand. Overcome with a tremendous sense of loss, he set about reforming his personal behavior. Graeme's death had served a positive purpose, after all.

Duncan could see bullying as a dead end, with no friends, and always having to look over his shoulder to be sure someone bigger hadn't spotted him as potential prey. Violence and cruelty were the only types of social interactions he had become familiar with. He started watching and listening to how others engaged. He learned about nonverbal communication: smiles and nods and shrugs, removing a cap before speaking, and, in general, he practiced good behavior. In no time, he found himself expressing thanks and speaking in a normal tone to others. The unhealthy need for threats and intimidation were something to be kept in the past. He began to feel good about himself. New to this area of Scotland, he had no established reputation to overcome and was able to start fresh in his relationships. He wanted to be liked and thought of as able to be counted on by others.

Amazingly, this changed mindset enabled the relationship with his family to flourish. Annag depended on him more and more, sharing her innermost feelings and fears, an openness and tenderness with which Duncan had no experience. A novice in kind human interaction, he tried to absorb the situation despite having no basis on which to respond. In time, Duncan developed into a proper adult who valued the needs of others as well as his own personal needs. Others saw him as someone of value.

Duncan considered himself the caretaker of his mother and two sisters. Annag was proud of her son. Brighid and Moira worshipped him as only loving sisters can do, Brighid being four years younger than Duncan and Moira two years younger still. The Steel family showed them kindness. Nevertheless, Duncan saw the need for their own place, independent of the Steels, while enabling Annag to retain her employment with the family. This required Duncan to learn a trade and develop an income as the primary breadwinner, which Annag understood and supported.

On the family's next visit, Duncan reached out to Fiona Steel and politely inquired as to whether her husband could suggest a trade which showed promise for a young man. His request might be considered quite a bold step and its attainment perhaps beyond his class. Fiona understood this was merely outside the grasp of Duncan's social sensitivities. She smiled and said she would speak to Ian when she thought the time right.

For the next few weeks, Duncan did what odd jobs he could find in Paisley and the surrounding area. From shoveling coal to mucking stalls, moving furniture, and spading gardens—nothing was beneath the dignity of a young man trying to provide for his family.

One Saturday his work finished at midday; he returned to the Steel household and his mother and sisters. Annag, frantic, said a meeting had been arranged between Duncan and Ian Steel for the following day, after the noon meal. Duncan was thrilled at the prospect, while nervous since he had never met Ian Steel, only having heard his voice and seen him at a distance. Annag was so appreciative to Fiona for affording her son this opportunity and was hopeful of a good outcome. Brighid and Moira were nonplused at the excitement; they felt their brother was assuredly the best male person ever to grace western Scotland. They were certain of a successful meeting.

After a fitful night's sleep in the pantry room, Duncan and Annag and the sisters walked to church for an early service, so they would be back to the Steel household with time to spare before the scheduled meeting.

At the appointed time, Duncan entered the kitchen and was directed into the main house and to a room off the entrance foyer where Ian Steel kept an office. In this place, he saw visitors and conducted business when necessary. Duncan, nervous yet also confident, was overwhelmed at this opportunity for a person from his station. At the door, he looked in to see Ian Steel seated in a leather chair behind an enormous polished wooden desk. An oil lamp on the desk provided the room with a soft, warm glow, and Duncan saw shelf after shelf of bound books. On a far wall was a large oil painting of Fiona, Duncan guessed, as a beautiful younger woman.

Ian motioned to Duncan to come in and directed him to a seat next to the desk, facing the older gentleman.

Duncan started off right by thanking Mr. Steel for the meeting.

He nodded at the boy and smiled warmly, saying, "Mrs. Steel tells me you have aspirations."

Duncan looked blank, never having heard the word.

Ian covered for the disconcertion, saying, "Just tell me about yourself, in your own words."

Duncan sighed and put it all out there: the constant moving, the embarrassments, the bullying, the change in attitude, and the hope for a better future.

"I am trying to find a way to be able to provide for my mother and sisters, and thought you could assist me with some advice," said Duncan.

Ian Steel, impressed with the candor and honesty, could sense the innate optimism this boy had regarding life. After some more back and forth and penetrating questions, Ian determined Duncan Keillor had at least a minimal ability to read and write and knew his basic numbers. Ian explained about being a merchant in the wool trade. He bought wool, contracted with mills to spin and weave it, and then sold the finished product in the wholesale market. He had many contacts within the industry, and said he was sure he could find a commercial apprentice opportunity for an industrious young man. However, it meant working in Glasgow, with visits to his mother and sisters only on the weekends. He asked Duncan to think on it and come to his office in town at midweek for more discussion.

Duncan was overwhelmed and thanked his patron profusely.

Annag and the girls wanted to hear every detail and, surprisingly, weren't upset in the least about him living elsewhere. It meant more security for the three of them and the prospect of perhaps moving out into their own place. For the next few days, Duncan functioned in a kind of fog, faced with questions and decisions of the greatest import.

He went into Glasgow on Wednesday morning, his first trip to a large city, and waited for two hours to meet with Ian Steel, who apologized profusely about the delay. Another man with him in the office, introduced as Angus Bisset, was the general manager of Rowallan Woolen Mills in Glasgow. Angus said he was in need of a young person to support his commercial staff and, as a favor to Ian Steel, had come to meet Duncan. After the briefest of conversations, Duncan found out about an opportunity to learn the knitting business with Rowallan, which provided a starting wage plus room and board. Duncan could barely contain his excitement when Angus asked if he could start the following Monday. Ian sweetened the deal by offering to have him outfitted with more suitable clothing for office work, as a gift from his wife and himself.

Duncan said, "Y-yes!" and plans were made to transport Duncan to Glasgow on Sunday.

A proud Scottish boy literally flew home to tell his mother and sisters the great news. The next few days were a blur: Duncan was outfitted in new clothing, he placed some meager possessions in a well-worn loaned satchel, and rode a coach into Glasgow on Sunday evening. As he left, there were no tears from Annag or his sisters, and he made a promise to return the following Saturday afternoon. The office only worked a half day on the weekend and, of course, Sunday was a day of rest. Duncan had a letter directing him to a rooming house a few blocks from the Rowallan offices. His room was stark yet clean, with a soft bed and one dresser, a pitcher and wash bowl, plus a key to the common lavatory down the hall. A simple evening meal was always served family style in a dining room, and breakfast consisted of a buffet with oatmeal, breads, and fruit. He soon enjoyed some of the best nutrition of his young life.

On his first day of work, Duncan Keillor adopted a style which proved to be successful for him: head down, ears open, mouth mostly shut, like a sponge, absorbing thoughts, ideas, processes, rules—more information than a normal person could manage. He thrived on it. In time, he began to understand how the business operated and how the group he worked under fit into the overall scheme of things. For a poor boy with no exposure to the commercial side of life, this was an eye-opening experience. Understanding that his success directly linked to those he bolstered, he managed his own ego for the group's greater benefit. He became well liked and dependable, garnering positive comments and encouragement.

It was a happy day when he received his first pay envelope which contained some currency and coins. He kept an amount for himself to be able to buy lunch food during the midday break, and the remainder he proudly carried home to Annag. This first envelope provided enough funds for her to buy Sunday dresses for herself, Brighid, and Moira, an undreamed-of extravagance. What remained, she saved, hopeful to one day have a flat of their own. Duncan, giddy with his good fortune, stayed focused on doing his best in order to secure his future with the firm. This attitude and success were unique for someone from his station in life. He could not understand why he had been so blessed.

After a few months, Annag had saved an amount of cash enough to allow her to rent a flat large enough for her and the girls to have a space to call their own. Her wage from the Steels paid the rent and provided enough fire coal to keep them warm. When Duncan came back—no longer every weekend—he made a pallet on the floor in the common room that was comfortable enough, and they all were proud. Duncan went with them to Sunday worship at the Church of Scotland, walking behind Annag and holding hands with both his sisters. Annag fixed them a noon meal, and he regaled them with stories from the city and his work. Brighid was wide-eyed, while Moira focused on the reasons why he couldn't come back more often. They enjoyed the fruits of his labor. In the evening, he climbed into the coach going back to Glasgow.

One weekend, Ian Steel reached out to Duncan for a visit and, from behind the big wooden desk, told him of the very positive feedback he had received from Angus Bisset regarding his job performance. Ian had taken a risk on him and was glad things were working out so well. He counseled Duncan to stay steady and committed, and to think of Ian as someone he could turn to for advice. As the young man left, Fiona Steel patted his shoulder and smiled warmly, happy for his good fortune. This encouragement from the Steels stuck with Duncan for the rest of his life. He had been able to escape his reputation as "the son of the drunk."

The weeks stretched into months, and the months stretched into years. Duncan continued to provide for his mother and sisters, who were appreciative beyond belief. Duncan's hard work had enabled him to prosper, and he secured his own flat, of a couple of rooms, in a show of independence.

He still had no social life, focused solely on his advancement within the firm. He had enjoyed some education outside of the office. Using connections from Angus Bisset, he had been able to study factoring concepts with a bank, skills which he put to good use at Rowallan. He suddenly realized he now had a group of people under him and he truly added value to the firm. This work was recognized in the form of an increased wage, in addition to the boost he received when the firm no longer provided his room and board. He had a real future, but his life was all about work. He remained steadfastly anti-alcohol, so he did not join in with his peers when they went for a pint of ale or a whisky. Duncan had become a regular city churchgoer and this provided enough social interaction for the time being.

He went back to Paisley for a visit, having been away for several weeks. He still sent monies to Annag and his sisters, only now he did so via bank transfers, having outgrown the pay envelope long ago. When Annag answered the door following his knock, it shocked Duncan. Always thin, she was now shockingly so, with sunken cheeks and eyes which stared at him. She hugged Duncan, who could feel his mother's bones through her clothing as he lightly squeezed her. She had a sallow complexion, clearly in the throes of the late stage of some disease. Brighid and Moira stood nervously in the room, wringing their hands, as Duncan asked his mother what was wrong.

She sat down slowly at a table and sipped from a cup of tea. In a matter-of-fact tone, she said, "I am nearing my time."

The girls began to cry softly, and they sobbed out the story for him. Annag had begun to fail, and Mrs. Steel had arranged for a physician to examine her. In his judgement, she had a malignancy of the liver, much like Jesse McShanog long ago. Perhaps it ran in the family; he didn't know. The physician advised them to keep her comfortable and let nature take its course. Duncan, inclined to be angry at having been kept in the dark, understood their disinclination to interrupt his life. He appealed to Annag to come to Glasgow and be seen by other physicians. She said she felt too weak and resigned herself to her fate. She had come from nothing, an orphan, had a hard, brutal marriage, made a way for her family, and was now known as the mother of a prosperous young businessman from Glasgow. It was far more than she could have ever hoped for.

Annag passed on within the week, with her son and daughters by her side. She was laid to rest in the cemetery at the Paisley Abbey Church of Scotland, in a spare grave in the Steel family plot. This was a loving and graceful gesture from Fiona and Ian, in remembrance of her long service to them. Rowallan gave Duncan leave to handle her affairs and, anxious not to abuse this privilege, he sat his sisters down to decide how they wanted to proceed. No longer girls, they both had developed lives in the community and protested when Duncan suggested they come reside with him in Glasgow.

"This is our home," they both chimed in. "Please let us stay and live our lives."

Annag had managed to save a large portion of what Duncan had sent her and, together, they all agreed the girls should keep these funds as an emergency reserve. They both had jobs working in the municipal government center, a situation Duncan surely felt Ian Steel had had a hand in arranging. The girls were like surrogate daughters for the aging Steels and they filled the emotional void left by Annag's death. It would be a sentimental moment for Duncan, going back to the city, his home for some time now. With tears and hugs, the siblings parted with the realization that things never were to be the same. Life goes on, as they say.

In Glasgow, Duncan devoted himself even more to his career. He worked long hours, yet made sure he exercised and ate well to keep his strength and health. He gained more and more status and responsibility at the firm, where all was not smooth due to the vagaries of the wool markets, taxation from the government, attempts of labor to organize, and the stresses of life in general. Duncan thrived on these challenges and stayed mostly happy, save for an emptiness socially. Brighid and Moira stayed in touch with him regularly, both having many friends and prospects for marriage to share. They began to subtly pressure Duncan about his lack of a social life. Brighid, being older, was practical in her approach.

"The firm doesn't have any old bachelors. Does that tell you something?" she said to her brother, over a cup of tea one weekend when he was back in Paisley for a visit.

The more emotional Moira said, "You need someone other than us to love you!"

Duncan squirmed. Matters of the heart were emotions he was inexperienced with because of his circumstances. Thinking about it, he began to realize his insular approach to life might be seen by some as a weakness or a failing. His sisters encouraged him to be conscious of the need for interaction with the opposite sex, be it through church or business situations. It took initiative—which he clearly had in other aspects of his life. He smiled and realized they had challenged him in a manner which appealed to his need for accomplishment. He promised to make a special effort and update them as to how things were progressing. Aware that further pressure might have a negative result, the girls backed off and took a wait-and-see approach.

With his return to Glasgow, he began to make discreet inquiries with his fellow workers and a few respected superiors as to social opportunities for a person of his age and station in life. Because he handled the matter indirectly, it didn't seem like a plea for help. Rather, he was a young professional expanding his social horizons in a city still somewhat new to him.

In short order, Duncan began to frequent a veritable plethora of new and interesting venues: art exhibitions, dining clubs, dance academies, music halls, and the local theatre where one might be able to catch a bowdlerized version of Shakespeare. He made a stab at involvement in freemasonry, which he thought too clandestine and secretive. There existed a significant temperance movement, and he went to several talks and concerts promoted by the Abstainer's Union. He found the organization too political for his taste. In society at the time, an emphasis existed on "dancing and deportment"—very much in vogue with the younger women. Duncan invested time and money in lessons to learn the quadrilles, polkas, waltzes, and other carpet-style dances. Not overly light on his feet, he nonetheless became a competent, if not polished, dancer. In no time, Duncan Keillor became part of the social scene, the highlight of which was the Glasgow Fair, lasting a week in July each year.

The fair was an important happening in the general Glasgow area, which had business and community impact in addition to social aspects. Numerous consequential meetings were planned concurrent with the fair, to take advantage of the presence of people of importance from government, banking, law, business, and other decisionmakers. Although these affairs were a nudge above Duncan's current station, a prominent banker with ties to Angus Bisset and Rowallan approached the firm about putting forth an individual to attend a fundraiser for the Mitchell Library, a new institution sponsored by a wealthy Glasgow tobacco merchant. The event, a dinner and dance, was to be held in the rotunda of the copper dome of the library, and a table had been subscribed by the banker. The fundraiser was considered one of the finer events during Glasgow Fair Week, and the managing director of Rowallan felt it was a good opportunity for Duncan to get some exposure outside the firm, particularly since he had demonstrated some adept social skills. Recognizing this as a great honor, Duncan was so thrilled he sent word to Brighid and Moira so they could share in his good fortune.

The night of the dinner, Duncan took special pains to dress properly; he was not confident about semiformal attire. Most of his outfit was borrowed from others at the firm. He made sure his ghillie brogue shoes were shined, the belt and buckle polished, the sporran hung perfectly, the shirt was pressed, the kilt smoothed, and the jacket fitted properly. With a close shave and hair combed, he looked like a proper, prosperous Glaswegian and it made him feel good.

He took a public carriage to the library and was awed at the size and beauty of the structure. There were dozens of carriages, and he relaxed, enjoying the ride until his turn to disembark came about. Dressed not as formally as some—having no family fly plaid to show—he still felt confident as he strode up the broad stairs to the entrance. The rotunda was well lit by gaslights and candelabra. He nodded to the attendant and presented his invitation. He was escorted into the milieu of tables which gleamed with bright white tablecloths and napkins, sparkling stemware, lustrous china, and polished tableware. He stood by his chair and surveyed the scene, wiping back a tear as he thought of Annag and the girls. How proud they would be to see him at such an event! He made sure his place at the table had a water glass and then turned his wine goblets upside down.

He saw a string quartet playing music in front of a wooden dance floor on which a smartly dressed matron and her overweight husband tried the tango, a new Argentine dance which was gaining some interest. They failed miserably at the tango, but the others watching gave them a slight smattering of applause for the brave attempt. The crowd of mostly older people was more intent on consuming wine and spirits than dancing. The tables began to fill as the time for the introductory speeches approached, with the seat next to Duncan remaining vacant. He feared spending the evening talking to the late middle-aged woman next to him.

With no warning, the other men at the table suddenly stood, and Duncan followed suit only to notice a beautiful reddish-blond young woman take the open chair. She was perhaps a couple years younger than Duncan and so attractive as to render him tongue-tied for a moment. When she had been properly seated, he extended his hand and introduced himself. This was the moment Aileen Montgomerie came into his life.

The dinner served was sumptuous: smoked salmon, a creamy pâté, leek and potato soup with melting pats of butter, pheasant stuffed with carrots, and wedges of sharp, pungent cheese, followed by a scrumptious warm bread pudding. Aileen and Duncan chatted, each noticing the other's good table manners, while getting to know one another. Neither drank any alcoholic beverages, also noted. Both were out of their element at an event so formal and elegant and it made them a bit uncomfortable. Aileen was the niece of a friend of the banker who'd hosted the table, so the meeting may have been something of an arrangement. The pair hit it off famously. She was single, two years younger (although the identification of the age thing was danced around as maybe too prying), had never married, and lived on the far northern outskirts of Glasgow. A Presbyterian, she worked in a private bank, handling the paperwork associated with commercial transactions. She had greenish eyes, a fair complexion, and a trim, shapely figure. Duncan puzzled as to how such a comely lass as this was not yet married. They had only just met and this riddle needed some time to be solved.

After the meal, one last speech exhorted all to find a way to direct some monies into the trust which had been established to fund the operation of the library. Then the band began to play music suitable for traditional dancing. Aileen smiled at Duncan and said she fancied a dance now. Together they walked to the edge of the parquet. He took her hand and placed his arm around her waist as they began a graceful waltz. Sometimes, not often, dancing partners are made for each other. And so it happened with Duncan and Aileen. Their moves were so natural, relaxed, and syncopated with the music, you would have thought they had danced together for years. Gradually, others stopped dancing, to watch the two whirl away as if caught in a trance. When the music ended, they were the only two left on the floor, and the audience applauded enthusiastically, much to the embarrassment of the young couple. Aileen blushed. They sat at their table, where they chatted with enthusiasm until they became aware of the party winding down.

An older gentleman, attired in formal Scottish regalia, came to the table and reached for Aileen's hand as he said, "Seems as if you two had a lovely time."

Aileen responded, "Duncan Keillor, this is my uncle, Callum Montgomerie."

Duncan stood and gave the man a firm handshake. "I am pleased to spend such a delightful evening with your niece," he said.

Callum nodded and took Aileen's elbow, steering her away from the table.

She hesitated and said to Duncan, "I hope to see you again."

And thus began the courtship.

The following week, Duncan, besieged with messages from Brighid and Moira seeking details about the event, talked at length about the meal but was discreet about Aileen and the dancing. He didn't want things to get ahead of themselves. Around midweek, he slyly used office connections to obtain details about Aileen Montgomerie and her family situation. Her parents, Harry and Sandra, had perished in a fire when she twelve, and Aileen had been raised by her bachelor uncle and his housekeeper. The housekeeper had a family of her own and over the years had given Aileen only scant attention. Callum, although focused on his extensive banking interests, tried to be part of Aileen's life. Parenting was not something he had been prepared for, yet they managed. Aileen had developed a closeness with Callum, as if he were indeed her parent. Aileen appeared not to be too affected by the turmoil of life she had experienced, other than limited interaction with others her own age. Callum had engaged private tutoring rather than school for his niece. The library's social function was one of Callum's attempts to help expose her to others in a pleasant atmosphere.

Duncan was unsure how to proceed. Inexperienced in matters of courtship and sensitive to the protectiveness of Uncle Callum, against his better judgement Duncan decided to consult with Brighid and Moira. He took an afternoon off and arrived unannounced in Paisley by tram. The sisters were thrilled, both that he had interest in a female and that he valued their opinions. They decided he would invite Aileen to Sunday afternoon tea at a fashionable spot in Glasgow. Unsure of how to go about this, he did not want to ask her in person. Fearful she might decline, he took the coward's way out and sent a wire, addressed to her personally, to her banking office.

```
AILEEN,

PLEASE MEET ME THIS SUNDAY AFTERNOON AT
FOUR FOR TEA AT THE QUEEN STREET HOTEL TO
CONTINUE OUR CONVERSATION.

                    BEST REGARDS,
                    DUNCAN
```

He nervously stood next to the teletype, hopeful for a prompt reply.

Her quick response read: "Okay."

Duncan immersed himself in his work to keep his mind off the coming "date." He worked half a day Saturday and took the new tram to Paisley for some last-minute inspiration and encouragement from his sisters. He treated them to dinner and then arrived back in the city very late at night.

On Sunday, he dressed with particular attention to his appearance, attended church, and was at the Queen Street Hotel by three o'clock, an hour early. His sisters had warned him against overplanning, yet he wanted to be sure they had a private table well-suited for two. As he waited to speak with the head waiter, he sensed someone beside him. Turning, he was shocked to see Aileen, shyly smiling. She also had arrived early, fearful of being late. They shared nervous laughter and sat in the lobby, talking, until tea finally was served in the dining room. They had a delightful time and made plans to attend services at her church the next Sunday. This somehow was followed by a lunch hosted by Callum. And so began the courtship that delighted even the most tangentially involved observer.

Over time, Duncan impressed those with whom Aileen associated, most importantly, Uncle Callum. Callum had made discreet inquiries regarding Duncan Keillor and his prospects, with particular attention paid to the thoughts of Angus Bisset and Ian Steel. Duncan did not possess the family standing to reach the highest levels within the firm, while those who did depended on Duncan and were confident of his capabilities.

The relationship between the young couple blossomed into a warm love for one another. Neither had close friends and they developed a healthy co-dependence as they matured together. After a year or so, Duncan had made up his mind and told Brighid and Moira of his intention to marry Aileen. The girls had met her only a few times; still, they were thrilled at Duncan's happiness.

The following week Duncan approached Callum, seeking permission for Aileen's hand in marriage. Callum had grown fond—very fond—of Duncan, and was proud to offer his blessing to the plans. However, he felt Duncan needed to be made aware of a medical problem. Physicians had deemed Aileen likely barren, though they were unsure of the cause. Perhaps it was genetic or maybe even due to the stress over the loss of her parents. Regardless, Callum wanted Duncan to know so that if having children was of great importance, Aileen was not the one for him. Her uncle also hinted there may be other challenges due to her somewhat socially isolated childhood. Duncan was surprised, though not shaken by the news.

"A happy life with someone I love is the only prayer I hope to have answered," Duncan said.

Callum warmly embraced him and offered to pay for a wedding and honeymoon as his gift to them.

The next day, Duncan took Aileen to a park off Queen Street and, on a bench by a tinkling fountain, asked for her hand in marriage. Their subsequent kiss and embrace caused others in the park to stop and stare, it being so tender. Aileen was glowing.

Their wedding took place in early October in the chapel at the Church of Scotland near Callum's home, where Aileen had lived since her parents' untimely deaths. It was a modest affair in the front of the sanctuary, near the altar: the two of them and Callum, Brighid, and Moira. The sisters' spouses were in attendance, as well as people from both their workplaces. The guests were showing support for a marital union they were pleased with. After the service, they had a hosted meal in a room at the Bankers Club off George Square. Callum gave a lovely talk about how much Aileen meant to him and how happy he was she had found such a promising mate. Aileen blushed and gave her uncle a warm embrace. Everyone was delighted for the new couple. They spent their wedding night in the hotel on Queen Street where they'd had that first tea. It was a night of love for one another and their lack of experience in lovemaking made it ever the more tender. The next morning, they took a train for a trip of a few days, into the Highlands. They were embarrassed to be traveling together in public, yet it was one of the happiest times in either of their lives.

On their return to Glasgow, they moved into the flat Aileen had chosen as their first home. Since it was situated midway between Duncan's office and Aileen's bank, they were both able to walk to work. It was an adjustment for them, living with another person and learning each other's personal habits and quirks. Without broaching the subject of children, Aileen announced her intention to keep working for the foreseeable future. They shared the cooking and cleaning duties, though neither could be considered particularly proficient in the kitchen.

They dined out often on the weekends, able to enjoy the benefits of a double income—unusual for young couples of those times. Occasionally, they took a tram down to see Brighid and Moira and their growing families. Aileen relished being an aunt, and the sisters were happy their brother had found such an apparently perfect mate. About once a month, Callum hosted them for a dinner at his club. As neither had many interests outside of work, their time was spent focused on each other. They were regular worshipers at her lifelong Presbyterian church, and what social life they had revolved around work and their co-workers. They developed a strong reliance on each other and were happy with their lives.

Things went very well for three or four years. They could have afforded a much nicer, larger flat, while what they had met their current needs. They felt no social pressures to flaunt their success with a larger or more fashionable place. They were known and liked by the butcher, baker, and policeman alike. They were stalwarts of the neighborhood.

And then Callum took ill. He was a large man, and his years as a bachelor with a steady diet of beef, salt bacon, blood pudding, potatoes, eggs, soups, and rich desserts, combined with the fact that he had never met a haggis he didn't like, led to problems with high blood pressure. In his very late fifties, Callum had a stroke. He survived, suffering partial paralysis on his left side and severe aphasia, which impaired his ability to speak and communicate. No longer able to work, his business interests were liquidated. This devastated him, as work was his whole life, save his commitment to raising Aileen. She agonized for her uncle's plight. The housekeeper had no interest in functioning as a private nurse and promptly quit unceremoniously after some thirty-five years of continuous service to Callum. With Duncan's agreement, Aileen took leave from her job, deciding to dedicate herself to care for her uncle—a difficult responsibility.

Callum was frustrated with his situation; it was exacerbated by his inability to articulate his thoughts. With the left side of his face drooping and reddened, he nearly shook as he tried to get his words out. He could think them, so why couldn't he say them? Aileen reassured him, taking a damp cloth to his face, and offered encouragement, never showing a drop of pity while Callum's face contorted. Grateful for his niece's commitment to him, Callum squeezed her hand while a teardrop formed in one eye.

His care was a challenge: helping him eat, lifting the spoon to his mouth, wiping his chin as he drooled; changing his clothes; cleaning his messes; and offering continued emotional support. After work and on weekends, Duncan helped, giving Aileen a break from the strain and struggle. They traded night duty, and, after a time, the demands of the situation caused stress in their relationship. Duncan never wavered; nor did Aileen. This went on for several months and then, one day, Callum suffered another massive stroke and died in his bedroom, in the home where he had lived most of his life. It did not come as a shock to Aileen and Duncan; they had been aware of this probability. It was almost a relief that Callum was at peace.

The funeral was a quiet affair attended by Aileen, Duncan, his sisters, and Callum's business associates of long years in the banking business. Oddly, the housekeeper of many years did not come to pay her respects, either heartbroken or filled with rancor over some old or perceived slight. The minister spoke of Callum Montgomerie's life and the good works his money had enabled, including to the Church of Scotland. Callum's casket was then carried awkwardly out of the sanctuary by six old men who had for years called him friend. They took him down the steps, out into the cemetery beside the church, and laid him to rest.

Aileen, emotionally exhausted and devastated by the loss of her uncle, needed a long break. She spent the next few days dispersing her uncle's things to various charities, save a set of his favorite books he had wanted Duncan to have and some personal things associated with Aileen's parents.

Weeks later, in a barrister's office on Queen Street, the formal disposition of Callum's remaining assets were made known: Aileen received a sizeable inheritance; an equivalent amount went to the church; the housekeeper received a gift of cash and some sterling flatware that she had polished for years; and the remainder of the estate went to an organization which provided education and financial backing to victims of stroke. The inheritance was a mixed blessing for Aileen; it meant she never had to return to work, but outside of Duncan and Callum, work had been her life.

She struggled with how to move forward. The loss had a greater impact than expected. Former co-workers wished they had her kind of problems and said so, which further confused Aileen. For a while she drifted, unfocused and without motivation. Duncan did his best to support her emotionally, meanwhile getting back to performing well in his role for Rowallan. Things were at a place where emotions became held in suspension.

Days, weeks, and months went on. Winter became spring, then summer, then fall again. They shopped, talked, and tried to focus on their life together. They became regular attendees at the Church of Scotland, fending off attempts to place them in charge of various church offices or in leadership roles. By now they were in their late thirties, with Duncan well established at his firm and able to focus only on those business situations which interested him.

They enjoyed playing the role of city aunt and uncle to Brighid and Moira's growing families, traveling to Paisley for special holidays, birthdays, and the like. Duncan was secure in the knowledge of how proud Annag would have been over how things were turning out. He looked forward to the future.

And then Aileen began to change subtly. Nothing abrupt, mind you; there was no cataclysmic shift. Rather, it was a continuing metamorphosis. She slowly became more and more uncomfortable, suspicious of Duncan and his activities and, over time, a kind of negativity crept into every part of their relationship. Bewildered, Duncan protested her accusations, having to defend seemingly every spoken word which her frequent jealousy focused on. God forbid he be delayed in coming home from work. She ranted and raved, accusing him of lying, keeping secrets, giving others the attention that "was rightly hers and only hers." Out of nowhere, her face turned dark and scowling, followed by a rage over whatever insecurity haunted her at the time.

The neighbors had become accustomed to her shrieks of anger directed at a cowering Duncan—this was an odd change for a woman who had always been so calm and loving.

He sometimes slept on the floor of their kitchen because she had decided she could not stand the sight of him in their bedroom. Duncan's love for Aileen never wavered amid the hate which spewed from her like some bilious poison, yet the pain of her behavior caused irreparable damage to his psyche and their marriage.

Her condition continued to deteriorate, and Duncan never knew what to expect on returning from work each day. She went through periods of uncontrolled, irrational spending on things for which they had no use. She experienced binges, eating enormous quantities of foods, and then regurgitating out of guilt and resentment. She went through intense episodes of anger, depression, and anxiety lasting from only a few hours to days, with mood swings changing rapidly. Aileen could be relatively calm and then wildly change direction without warning, the triggers seemingly nonexistent. Life became a nightmare for both, with time apart from one another a comfort neither wanted nor understood.

What had begun as an emotional problem quickly became an out-of-control monster, and Duncan began to fear for his safety, such was the depth of Aileen's rage. Life for Duncan was reduced to walking on eggshells as he tried to find some level of interaction which permitted their relationship to continue, albeit frightful. Work became a refuge for Duncan; he kept to himself about his problems. This limited social interaction at the office provided a respite and preserved his sanity.

Their family and friends, noticing, did not understand the strain and tiredness were from a lack of quality sleep and chronic personal stress. They were sorry for how things were turning out for the couple, while thankful there were no children who had to suffer along with them.

The changing of the seasons did nothing to improve matters, and Duncan and Aileen's life continued to spiral into a chasm of terror: he afraid of her, and she afraid of something she couldn't articulate or understand. She became more and more isolated and seldom left the flat. At times like these, Duncan went out of his way to say things to soothe her and assuage her fears, but nothing helped. He became the family grocery shopper, picking up their needed items on his way home from work each day. Occasionally, there were brief periods approaching normalcy which suddenly and forcefully ended in arguments and yelling and name-calling and rages from Aileen. Though the episodes were physically and emotionally challenging for Duncan, he remained committed to her and their marriage, perhaps out of a fear of their marriage ending in failure, as his parents' had.

Today we would say Aileen suffered from deep depression or, perhaps, more darkly, a serious personality disorder. In those times, it was termed *melancholy* and presumed to be a personal failing and weakness. Serious mental disorders were not well understood. The associated behaviors were not recognized as an involuntary response to certain conditions rather than those which could be controlled or minimized—well before medications were even thought of to manage anxiety, depression, paranoia, and other emotional maladies. In most cases, patients were ostracized, isolated, and otherwise marginalized by society in general, and by the medical profession in particular.

In any regard, the result of her condition would perhaps be tragic, ultimately leaving her loving husband alone to deal with her final desperate devolution, and not something he could have foreseen or even imagined, it being beyond the scope of his sensibilities.

Nothing prepares one for dealing with tragedy within a family. It came without warning or any trigger anyone could have anticipated or understood. Late one afternoon, Duncan was away at work. On an impulse, Aileen spotted a bare chair in the corner of the bedroom of the lonely apartment, the one Duncan sat on each morning as he pulled on his trousers while preparing for work and whispering for her to please feel better and have a good day.

Damn him! What did he know about the darkness which swallowed her most every day, the malignant spirits crushing every single bit of hope from her ravaged soul?

She dragged the chair into the hall and positioned it a certain way. She climbed onto it, reached up and tied off the thick cord to the light, and thence her neck. She smiled broadly for the last time. For once, she felt totally in control of her situation.

Before suppertime, arriving home from another trying day at Rowallan, Duncan found Aileen hanging from a gaslight in their dark flat, a chair knocked askew nearby. It was clearly not an accident. He surveyed the scene, choking back sobs as tears streamed down his cheeks. His worst fear was realized, and the months of emotional turmoil had reached their end. Duncan untied the rope from around Aileen's neck and tenderly laid her body on the wooden floor of the hall outside their bedroom, covering it with a favorite blanket pulled from their bed. No discoloration had formed in her face or extremities. He didn't want her beauty to be destroyed by the selfish act of suicide she had left him to deal with. He loved his wife and wanted her to be remembered only as positively as possible by those who knew her. This kindness was what he owed her—he not being like his father.

Duncan wept beside her body for the longest time, unable to accept what could possibly have brought their lives to this point, after the beginnings of such a promising marriage. Duncan was jolted out of his haze of grief by the sound of evening church bells pealing in the distance, something which had oddly never been noticeable to him before this day. He thought perhaps this a call from God. He went to the kitchen basin, lifted the pitcher, and poured water into the bowl, fascinated by the sound of the splashing. He washed his face with his hands, and the cool water settled him. He dried himself on a towel which Aileen had embroidered in happier times. After a while he went out of the apartment, locking the door, to go fetch the minister. He didn't want to leave her alone, yet he did what he had to do.

Things became something of a blur for Duncan. Brighid and Moira fought through their own grief and were of great help to him, seeking to handle several decisions about the funeral arrangements and discussions with the authorities. There were some difficulties associated with formally recording her death, and the church made it burdensome to bury her in Callum's funeral plot due to the way it appeared her life had ended. Angus Bisset, by now a very old man, was enraged over the conduct of the local church and used his considerable influence in the presbytery to quickly rectify things. Duncan's colleagues at Rowallan provided emotional support and reassurance. Throughout, Duncan remained stoical and resolved in his efforts to be sure Aileen was remembered for the gentle manner she had been known for in her younger years, although there was no denying that things had been tough over the last year.

For some time, Duncan went about the business of trying to return to a normal life. In Scottish society, grieving had certain expectations associated with it. Because their lives had always been so private and they were so young, others didn't know exactly what type of behavior to expect or demand from Duncan. Everyone grieves differently, yet there are patterns society tends to share. Initial shock, followed by guilt, anger, and denial are common responses. They are often followed by a lack of interest or energy. The passage of time permits one to move through an emotional process leading towards acceptance and healing. Unfortunately, Duncan never recovered from Aileen's tragic suicide. Eventually, as time passed, a kind of emotional scab formed as Duncan went about the process of trying to heal himself. His work at Rowallan had not become the saving grace his friends had hoped for. Very sharp intellectually, he still possessed an ability to create innovative approaches to commercial challenges, though none of it mattered to him. In the scheme of things, he saw work as an end, a way of helping one's self, not something having intrinsic value in and of its own right.

Duncan's focus began to shift ever so slightly. He took long walks away from the office, particularly in the afternoons when cold rains swept inland, off the Irish Sea. In a long overcoat, he huddled under a black umbrella. The hiss of the falling drops of water seemed to soften things. He kept to himself, neither recognizing nor nodding to others as he passed. Sometimes he stopped and gazed into shop windows. He did not show any emotion—almost like walking in a trance, trying to decide what to do with the rest of his life. His ownership interest in the firm would likely enable him to have a normal lifestyle in perpetuity, albeit void of extravagance. Continuing to go into the office was a grasp at normalcy, rather than a need to generate income or to advance his career. He had no interest in remarrying—having proven, at least in his own eyes, to be sadly lacking in the skills of being a mate. The apartment had so many reminders of Aileen and their troubles as her life spun out of their control that he no longer felt comfortable there. Then again, where might he feel comfortable, or could that even be possible? He didn't recognize these feelings as being based in grief; rather, this was his life now and he needed to begin the job of repairing himself.

He had once heard a philosopher state, "No one can help anyone else; you need to help yourself!"

Though not sure he believed this statement, Duncan understood the need to take charge if he was ever to become a productive, emotionally stable person again.

And so, one afternoon on his walk, he came to a park square not far from Rowallan's offices and sat down on a bench. There weren't many leaves left on the sycamores which loomed over the park. Some boxwood hedges nearby were still green and fragrant. It made an altogether pleasant space. The rain had stopped, at least for a while, and he collapsed his umbrella. He leaned back and took a deep breath of the moist air. Since it was late afternoon, a few shops had their gaslights on, which cast a soft glow on the damp pavement. He noticed people moving about, mostly in a hurry to get somewhere. A young mother pushing a child in a pram came by and she smiled at him, mouthing the words "Good evening." He smiled back and then, as she moved on, he began to lose his composure. Sobbing, he placed his face in his hands and had a good cry, and then shook his head, wiped his eyes, and smiled again. His emotional recovery from the loss of Aileen began from this point.

He decided to seek out the counsel of Brighid and Moira, who both were in the process of raising families of their own. He hired a private carriage down to Paisley and hosted his sisters at tea in the hotel where he normally stayed overnight. The girls, young women now, so loved their brother and were indebted for his years of taking care of them. His anguish and sadness over the loss of Aileen was heartbreaking for them.

He told them of his ideas for a path forward with his life, wanting to seek out opportunities where he could help others who were dealing with problems of the type which overwhelmed young people: examples included alcohol, family abuse, economic misfortune, and dealing with various types of mental illness and troubles of the psyche. He had some ideas for how to approach the people and the issues, something in which he could perhaps feel enthusiasm again.

The sisters eagerly encouraged their brother. How could they not? Before he left, they each enjoyed a final embrace of the sort experienced by those who have endured shared sacrifice together.

Duncan Keillor, the "bully boy of Ayrshire," commenced to become a lifelong missionary of sorts. He never remarried or ever earned a paycheck again, taking permanent leave from Rowallan. Instead, he lived out his life traveling and working in many cities and towns, large and small, throughout western Scotland. He carried a valise with some extra clothes, toiletries, and a Bible. He provided elemental aid to emerging social service efforts and organizations, trying to make things better for those with problems.

While Duncan never had any formal training—save his life experience—he intuitively knew how to differentiate between those he could help and those who were best helped by others such as the church or local government. He understood the problems were not only with the individual affliction, but also with the way society reacted to those so afflicted.

Over time, he began to focus on those who were suffering mental or emotional challenges. Walking from town to town in all sorts of weather, he developed a method of going into the center of the village or city and asking for an area where individuals with problems tended to congregate. Today we might say he looked for "street people." The reality was that those homeless people represented only the beginning. He reached out to town authorities, ministers and priests, and others in a position to be aware of those with mental challenges. When he found the victims, he talked with them and showed understanding, reaching out to their families, trying to be an advocate for those who couldn't represent themselves. He had limited success. Duncan was often rejected by those who were troubled, and was told to mind his own business by families who reacted to the problems of their loved ones with embarrassment and shame. Realistic about being limited in his ability to help them heal, he focused on helping them find warm shelter, regular food, and a safe environment. Attitudes of the public shocked him and, many times, he witnessed emotionally challenged people being tormented by groups of children—often in the presence of other adults. He met anger and insult with kind words and encouragement. This was not a contest; any individual he helped was another person better off.

Duncan was not a feel-good evangelist, but rather a worker, organizer, and listener, sharing common experiences and trying to bring about a change in societal attitudes. He visited newspaper editors, union halls, church functions, library gatherings, county fairs, athletic events, bake and livestock sales, and local elections, any place where he could find a group of people and a forum to engage them. He was often met with skepticism or the belief that he could be some type of confidence man. Over time, he started to get some positive recognition, which grew when others took up the cause he championed. He seldom slept in the same place two nights in a row, constantly following any opportunity to share his message while helping those who had lost their way. Sometimes he slept in a church pew, or a basement, or a barn loft; a few times he even slept in a doorway. He normally paid for his meals, sometimes helped by locals who looked kindly on what he tried to accomplish. Duncan spoke with such candor and so from his heart that people simply gave him time to have his say.

The late nineteenth century was a time of economic turmoil in Scotland, which made his efforts more difficult. Duncan felt his cause to be proper. He never resorted to sharing the story of Aileen and her troubles. In his mind she another victim, one he still loved dearly, and her problems were between the two of them; they were not something he wished to exploit. While his efforts took a physical and emotional toil personally, to him they were a labor of love.

After a while, he became something of a political force in western Scotland. His opinion was sought and favored by those with influence and in positions of power. Whether he was a catalyst or simply in the right place at the right time, Duncan noticed attitudes began changing and troubled people began to get assistance and understanding across society, in even the most remote of locales. He saw progress, but felt his work never to truly be done. There would always be those who could still benefit from his advocacy. And so he continued his journey, keen to do the work he felt as a calling rather than a mission.

Communication in those days was informal and often by word of mouth, and rarely from newspapers. Presbyterian and Catholic communities embraced him. His stops became expected and welcomed. Modest as always, he declined recognition as well as offers of financial aid, although the odd meal and use of a bed were always welcomed. He felt his work right and was energized with the knowledge of honoring his personal memory of Aileen.

Once or twice a year, his travels took him near Paisley, and Brighid and Moira got to see him. He took pride in the loving families his sisters had raised and their solid marriages gave him great happiness. When together, they talked of Annag and how pleased she would have been, and, likewise, they remembered the good times with Aileen.

The years of travel began to take their toll on Duncan. Worn out by years of commitment and personal sacrifice, he resided for a few months one winter with Brighid and her husband Gordon, in Paisley. While there, he succumbed to heart disease.

His sisters held a local church service, and had Duncan laid to rest in Glasgow, in the Presbyterian cemetery next to Aileen, the only love of his life. He was mourned by those whose lives he had touched.

*Chòrr ann an sìth,*˙ Duncan Keillor, the bully boy of Ayrshire.

˙*Chòrr ann an sìth* is Scottish Gaelic for "Rest in peace."

# The Old Speckled Hen

eeping his tone even, Colly said, "I'm asking you one
more time, nicely, to head out the door and leave my
establishment."

The young oaf stood facing the bar, arms down, fists balled,
teeth clenched, and face red with rage and embarrassment. "Not
until I finish me beer that I paid you for!" he shouted back.

Colly replied, "Sophia, take his beer and give him back his money."

Then Colly reached under the bar and pulled out a club made
of wood and lead, wrapped in leather. He laid it on the bar for
everyone to see. He gazed coldly at the young tough, who wisely
took some coins the barmaid had placed on the bar, and quickly left.
Colly nodded and mouthed a word of thanks as Graeme righted the
stools that had been knocked over. Order was restored in The Old
Speckled Hen once again.

William Collins was born poor in Dalry, Ayrshire, as the only
child of George and Agnes Collins. George toiled as a coal miner at
the Blair Mine. Agnes was a chambermaid for a laird, a landowning
entrepreneur from Glasgow who maintained a country home near
Dalry. Agnes's only pregnancy had been difficult, with much sickness
and misery. After a very hard and long labor, William came forth. He
could have been considered a runt, if you will; he was tiny in stature

They saw too many workers, particularly miners and weavers, destroy their families' livelihood through uncontrolled consumption of stout ale, whisky, and wine, resulting in crushing poverty and wasted lives. Their son, now in his late teens, of a slight build, was not suited for physical labor, and opportunities in Dalry for work using your brain rather than your back were rare. They decided to speak with their pastor on Sunday afternoon, before raising the issue with Colly.

The pastor, Norman, listened intently over tea in his office at the Kilbirnie Auld Kirk Church of Scotland, outside Dalry. He weighed their concerns about earning a wage in an alcohol establishment and the lack of local opportunity for a person with physical limitations. Agnes did most of the talking, while George wordlessly fixed his eyes on every muscle movement in the pastor's face, desperate for some indication of his true feelings.

After a bit of silent thought, the pastor cleared his throat and spoke. Surprisingly, he was enthusiastic. He felt this was a real chance for Colly, particularly because it involved the laird, a sometime attendee at services and a large financial contributor of the church.

"The laird is a fair man, and I suspect that his support, in large measure, will result in a favorable outcome for your son."

He patted both their hands and said they were good parents. It was time for Colly to make some decisions on his own. The same evening, over a simple meal of soup and crusts of bread, George and Agnes laid out the opportunity for Colly, emphasizing both the positives and the negatives. They mentioned the pastor had suggested that many in the congregation viewed beer as harmless, nutritious, and even healthy.

The conversation slowed and, quietly chewing, Colly looked at them without blinking. Nodding, he said he would be "happy for the chance."

They agreed to remain quiet until things were sorted out—less they spoil the good fortune. Agnes spoke to Fraser the next day.

Word came back to the effect that the pleased laird hoped to return in a few days.

The following Saturday, Colly dressed in his best clothes and brushed his ginger-red hair straight back to make himself appear taller. At midday, he shook his father's coal dust–stained hand and walked down the well-traveled road to the laird's home, where his mother waited nervously. He kissed her on the cheek, she whispered some tender words of encouragement, and Colly went into the study of the laird.

They talked briefly, and then Fraser fetched the horse-drawn carriage. Together, they rode into town in the cool damp air, leaden clouds floating barely above the rooftops, and stopped in front of "The Old Speckled Hen." And things were never the same for William Collins ever again.

The driver opened the door, and the two walked into the pub, referred to locally as the "Hen." Inside, the laird introduced Colly to Fiona, who ran the place.

"This is the lad we discussed," said the laird. "He has my support."

He nodded, strode out to his carriage, and left the two of them alone. Though it was a bit of an awkward situation, Fiona knew she needed to make this work.

Hands on her hips, she looked him over and down, smiled and held out her hand. "Welcome. Now, let's get to work."

The Hen, known as a free public house, which inferred private investment (as opposed to those commonly referred to as tied houses that were owned by brewing consortiums), served a local clientele plus any travelers who happened by. There were four areas on the ground floor, featuring a bar, or serving room, with a line of beer engines—devices which pumped beer, ale, porter, stout, and cider from barrels behind the bar. Some bottles of whisky, gin, wine, and fortified wine lined a shelf. Next was a large room with tables and chairs where food was consumed—seemingly in need of a good cleaning. Additionally, there was another room which looked like it could be used as a meeting place. It was fitted with a dartboard and a table set for whist or dominoes, and a kitchen in the back. A stone floor went throughout, covered with a layer of sand to catch spills. The upstairs had two rooms: a bedroom and an office. The meager furnishings in the bedroom consisted of a bed frame and mattress and a dressing chair, while the office held a desk with a chair, an iron safe, and a simple table. Public lodging wasn't offered, officially; Fiona and her husband had kept the second-floor room as a place to rest from time to time. The only light came from windows, candles, oil lamps, and the reflected flames from the fireplace. The temperature was kept comfortable and the place had a relaxed, worn feel.

In the pub, only a customer or two were deep in conversation with a plump barmaid. Fiona motioned to a table away from the bar. She poured herself a cup of tea and began a conversation with Colly.

"The Hen started many years ago as an enterprise of my parents, Fergus and Maldy M'Kenzie. They ran the place for years, and I worked here … cleaning, washing, serving, and doing whatever needed to be done. We made a good living and stayed in a tenement apartment down the street. When Gordon McMurdo and I married, he worked in the mine, with no prospects. We took over the place from Mum and Dad, and we, too, enjoyed a good life. Then Gordon got the bloody cough and couldn't work or even eat much, for that matter. I tried to run the place and take care of him best I could, but things got away from me. And then Gordon passed."

A tear formed on her cheek, and she wiped it away with her hand.

She shook her head and said, "Life has to go on. The place about went 'tits up,' and I went through trouble paying the bills. The laird stepped in, bless him, and put in an investment. He felt the town needed a pub the working class could call their own. I will manage the customers, but I need you to manage the business affairs of the place."

A bit taken aback, Colly took note of the fact that he had no business experience. Always keen with numbers, he did know right from wrong and figured to give it a go, seeing how things worked out.

He climbed the stairs to the office and saw a mess of strewn papers, a chair, and a writing table. The safe, with the door wide open, was empty, save for a few coins. He took off his jacket, rolled up his sleeves, and set about trying to organize things.

What records that existed were sloppy and entries infrequent. He soon figured out that the place operated hand to mouth, with a common pot of money and no real plan as to income and outgo. Regulations associated with the pub's license from the Crown required records to be kept, hours of operation to be observed, and submission to regular inspections of both the facility and the books. Colly saw no way to pass any inspection unless he fabricated documents, which he proceeded to do, absent any discussion with Fiona—his first, big, risky decision. At midday, he helped himself to some soup and a crust from the kitchen, and then he began to take a general inventory.

The physical plant of the Hen was sound: the building solid; thatched and slate roofs secure; furniture adequate; beer engines functioning; kitchen properly vented; mutchkins, or pint containers, in good numbers; and quantities of ale, beer, stout, wine, and cider enough to maintain a brisk trade. The whisky was very limited; it included some locally produced poteen which, though tasty, was not officially approved for sale due to regulation. There were teapots, some pewter plates and wooden spoons, the odd knife, and cups made of a ceramic-like substance. All proved adequate for a meal service. The kitchen consisted of a fireplace with a griddle and a clay oven beside it, and a brick hearth in front of it. A tub and buckets provided means for minimal cleaning of plates and utensils.

Colly figured that improved cleanliness would add to the meal trade and give the place a more comfortable look. As night fell, the pub, which closed by eight o'clock per regulation, sighed with weariness. Colly approached Fiona, who was standing by the bar with a vacant look. He took the damp cloth from her hand and carefully wiped the bar with some loving strokes.

He smiled and said, "My lady, I think we will be fine."

In a short time, they developed something of a ritual. After closing each night, Colly swept the sand—adding a few ladles to spots needing it, checked the bar top for cleanliness, snuffed out the candles, and locked the door behind him. Fiona developed trust in him and left each evening after the meal service, repairing to a set of rooms she and Gordon kept over the years in a tenement a scant two blocks down the street. Colly buttoned his coat tight against the evening chill and walked to his folks' home. Sometimes they stayed awake and waited for him, eager to share in his stories of the day.

In Dalry, a town where everyone knew most everyone else, local gossip was clearly a sort of entertainment regularly enjoyed. To his credit, Colly did not betray confidences, yet shared with his parents, in good fun, humorous anecdotes about some of the characters who frequented the Hen. The bar catered to a broad, non-elitist clientele, save for the laird and some of his infrequent cronies. Pubs provided a service to the community, offering emotional support, friendship, and a source of information. The Hen became a trusted location where those new to the area could meet others of like circumstance and receive assistance in finding work and lodging. With Colly helping to run the Hen now, those from the lower or working class felt comfortable spending some time and money in its club atmosphere—confident not to be taken advantage of.

In those days, in that part of western Scotland, drinking establishments were informally monitored by Presbyterian ministers who opposed whisky, yet saw beer as a more wholesome drink. Fiona and Colly found this contradiction offensive; looking down on clientele was not something they tolerated. In short order, the Hen became known as a place where one felt comfort and safety, as opposed to the infamous shabeens, or unlicensed places, where methylated spirits and other illegal liquors caused drunkenness and fierce abuse of alcohol. Not to say some people weren't sometimes overserved to the point of judgement impairment at the Hen, but Fiona and Colly kept their eyes open. Such situations were rare and were handled discreetly.

Over time, an informal relationship with some of the regulars evolved. A few served as "enforcers," to assist in minimizing disorder and make sure criminals or ruffians were quickly shown the door. The local justice of the peace controlled licenses, and it was good business to be seen as running a clean house. While some places encouraged trollops and prostitutes, Colly figured they were not worth the clientele they attracted. He gently let them know they were not welcome.

As a free house, the Hen could offer whatever brand and quality best served their clientele. While this changed with the times, in most cases one or two engines were dedicated to cheap "two penny" ale, another to a fine Glasgow porter, and the rest alternated between various ciders, stouts, and beers. Normally they offered a selection of whisky, wine and fortified wine, and, rarely, some Irish mead—a honey-based spirit—when outsiders were expected. Mead never kept long and spoilage could not be risked.

Time passed, and Colly became more and more proficient in operating the whole place. He handled the selection of beverages and food menus, always with a nod from Fiona as he developed his confidence. Fiona gradually deferred to Colly, challenging him to help expand his experience and build his self-assurance. She had taken to giving herself some time off, a morning or afternoon here and there. She also involved him in the hiring, and infrequent firing, of the wait and kitchen staff.

Fiona kept a hard eye out for people and possessed the innate knowledge that good people should be kept happy if the place were to be successful. With cooks, you simply ate their food, it being either good or time for a new cook. Kitchen help had to be self-managing, knowing and doing the necessary to keep things flowing smoothly. The barmaids needed to be pleasant and clean, if not attractive, and above theft or giving away beverages, without exception. Some of the buxom girls with cheeks like a milkmaid's thought they could appeal to Colly's masculine side and tried flirting or showing him a bit too much flesh, an area where Colly exhibited absolutely no weakness. He had total self-control. Fiona smiled knowingly, watching Colly carefully and deftly put the girls in their place.

"That Colly, he has a gift for saying no in a way that don't hurt no one," she was fond of saying.

After a year and a half, Colly was pretty much in charge of the Hen. The books were in order, the place operated smoothly, and things could be called "stabilized." The laird asked for a meeting of the three of them, in order to try and forge a path forward. While things were stable, the profits were still not sufficient, in the laird's mind, and he felt they needed to be creative. Fiona, on the other hand, felt things were good and she wanted to find some way to ease out of a daily role so she could enjoy life a bit more.

By now, Colly knew he had a real talent for running the establishment and needed to take care of himself over the long term. George and Agnes were getting along in years, and he wanted to be able to provide them a means to semiretire. It was an interesting concept, since in those times you normally worked until you were unable to, from either weakness or sickness, and forced to go "on the dole." Colly wanted the couple to be able to enjoy life before things got to that point, and he was the only possible means to provide it. At twenty-two years old and ambitious, he sought a way, over time, to gain ownership of the Hen from the laird and Fiona. They both were incredulous when he spoke of his plan, and thought such an idea impossible for someone of his young age. They had learned not to underestimate Colly, however, and were prepared to listen.

Colly pretty much figured out that beer and ale offered limited profitability. Beer was a commodity readily offered by others in comparable quality and cost, and was managed in large part by the brewers who established prevailing prices through their control of the tied houses. While fine porters, whisky, and wine were more profitable, they were limited by how much quantity the local market had the capacity to absorb.

The Hen was not the only pub in the Garnock Valley, yet it was the most convenient. It had to protect its competitive position in the market, sitting on the road from Glasgow, to Ardrossan and Saltcoats on the coast. To increase the trade through the pub, he needed to enhance the reputation of the place and bring in more customers. Colly thought maybe food could be the answer. He developed a scheme to expand the kitchen and turn the meeting room into more of a dining place. Their traditional "pub grub" included crude meat pies with vegetables, pork "snatchings" (rinds), pickled eggs in earthenware crocks, crisps (a kind of shaved fried potato), and a local favorite sot (a dish made from fermented cabbage and potatoes, kept in a tub under the bar and spooned onto a plate, with an oatmeal cake). This trencherman-type food was filling, inexpensive, and not very profitable.

What Colly envisioned in addition to, rather than a replacement of, the existing fare, included a menu with an array of sandwiches on thick bread: egg, cheese, salted beef, tongue, liver, mutton, boiled chicken, and pork. On Friday nights, he regularly offered a fresh haggis, a traditional delicacy made from a sheep's pluck (heart, liver, and lungs), and cooked in the stomach from the same animal. He served it steaming from the oven. Maybe add a black pudding, deep-fried blood sausage, a Scotch pie featuring double-crusted minced mutton or a kidney pie with diced onions and brown gravy in a pastry crust. And he offered platefuls of fresh oysters, in season, both on the shell and in creamy stews. As special orders, he potentially hoped for baked hare and pheasant.

His imagination ran wild—until he realized he needed to add to the menu over time. He sought to determine a value of the business in its current state and use the income that exceeded that to pay off the business partners over a time horizon, at the end of which Colly would become the principal owner. Fiona and the laird would receive, in addition, a monthly dividend for some time thereafter.

Fiona was all for it, but the laird hemmed and hawed over the arrangement. While happy with Colly's performance and initiative, the laird saw him as an employee rather than a partner. The laird and Fiona were dependent on Colly; should he choose to go elsewhere to work, they might suffer greatly. They made some adjustments in the sums and the time periods, and, for the most part, the plan which Colly had developed ended up accepted.

George and Agnes were so proud of their son becoming an independent businessman, and excited at the real prospect of easing into retirement over some future time frame. A few days later, during a late dinner in their kitchen, Agnes and George broached the subject of Colly moving out on his own.

George said, "Son, you will have a bed in our home whenever you need or want it."

Colly saw a tear forming in his mum's eye as she nodded in agreement.

Truth be known, Colly had been thinking of the very same thing for some time. So, amidst the other changes in his life, he decided to move into the spare room on the second floor of the Hen. In it were a bed, of sorts, and a table with a candlestick. He found an old dresser at Fiona's place that had belonged to her parents. She gave it to him to use, plus a bowl and pitcher on a stand with an alcove beneath in which to hide a chamber pot. Both the office and the sleeping room each had a door which provided necessary privacy. It meant spending most of his waking and sleeping hours in the Hen; if this were to work as he planned, he needed to dedicate himself. Fiona also contributed a feather bed ticking, and Agnes provided a set of bed linens and towels. He moved an extra hat tree from the pub downstairs, into a corner where he could hang his coat and hat. It made for a nice home and although he had no window views for relaxation, many nights he found himself lulled to sleep by the sound of rain splashing on the slate roof.

During the time he spent at the Hen, Colly saved quite a bit of money, having not much to spend it on except for contributions to his parents. He lived out of the place, taking most of his meals there, and avoided sampling the various alcoholic beverages— feeling he needed to always keep his wits about him. He took some of his cash and purchased a new, large cast-iron stove with two ovens. It was constructed to be fueled by coal, with a large hot water tank situated along the backside. He also bought three wash-rinse tubs arranged on a stand for proper cleaning of the new earthenware plates, saucers, and cups he ordered. In addition, he secured metal utensils with bone handles: knives, forks, and spoons. He reluctantly stayed away from glass due to expense and the risk of breakage. He got the stove provider to kick in, at cost, a new set of pots and pans, enabling the Hen to rival the finest restaurants in Glasgow.

The next Saturday, he walked to the laird's house and asked Fraser to speak to his partner. Fraser, only slightly put off by the question, in short order showed Colly into the laird's study. It was after lunch. The laird, in his red velveteen jacket, was smoking a cigar and watching the smoke curls while enjoying a pot of tea.

"I want your help, sir," Colly said politely.

He explained they needed professional talent in the kitchen if they were to be successful in building their food business.

Colly added, "Not necessarily a real chef, but certainly something more than a cook."

The laird indicated a chair for Colly to sit on.

Quiet in thought, the laird rolled the cigar on his lips, licking the flavorful tobacco, and said, "I have an idea."

The laird mentioned Andrew, a school chum of years past, having an interest in a fine restaurant in Paisley, near to Glasgow.

"I will inquire as to whether someone junior in his kitchen may have the potential to step in and run a new place."

This relieved Colly, and he walked back to the Hen for the evening rush, confident in making progress.

In a few days, the laird had a chat with his friend, over some fine whisky at their gentlemen's club in Glasgow. After some chitchat, the laird got to the point, explaining to Andrew his predicament. Submitting himself to some good-natured ribbing about owing favors, Andrew offered to arrange for a meeting with the candidate in Dalry for the laird and his partner, Colly.

The day came and, at midday, they were introduced to Cairstine Watts.

Cairstine, or Cairie, as she preferred, was in her mid-twenties and had been in kitchens for nearly ten years, having recently worked her way up at several restaurants to what might be termed a sous-chef, or second in command. Not married and her parents not involved, she had dedicated herself to becoming a successful chef. In food circles at this time, accomplished cooks commonly were somewhat itinerant, moving from place to place as they learned their craft and built reputations. Before Paisley, she had worked in two places in Glasgow and one in Dumbarton, each with increasing levels of responsibility. While the population of Dalry made her uncomfortable, out of respect for Andrew she had agreed to attend the meeting.

The laird and Colly were a bit taken aback on meeting her since they had expected a male rather than a female. Colly nodded at her concerns and proceeded to share with Cairie his dream of turning The Old Speckled Hen into something of an area food destination, a must stop for travelers coming to or from the southern coast of Scotland. He described the investment in the facilities and his ideas for developing a menu.

Cairie listened politely, and the laird suggested a carriage ride to view the Hen. Colly proudly trekked her through the pub, his enthusiasm infectious. Cairie folded her arms and asked some questions, particularly about potential suppliers of foodstuffs, meat, milk, vegetables, and so forth. The place, not as small as she had been afraid of and not as large as she had hoped for, did have potential. Colly voiced concerns that the current kitchen staff not feel threatened, as they had been loyal, although he affirmed Cairie had charge of managing the kitchen. Fiona had given her proxy to the partners in the knowledge it could hasten her move away from the business. The laird nodded to Colly, who swiftly made Cairie an offer of employment. Aware that chances like this didn't often come along, Cairie didn't hesitate and they struck an agreement.

It took a couple of weeks for Cairie to extricate herself from the restaurant in Paisley. During this time, Colly broached the change with the kitchen staff, who all reacted positively. This development provided hope for a solid future with the commitments the owners were making. Fiona stepped in and made an offer to Cairie of the use of a room in her flat, both to help her ease into the community and to provide Fiona some needed companionship.

News of the change spread by word of mouth. However, it took time to establish the new menu and improved venue. While still a pub, there were great expectations of the Hen for an improved dining experience.

Cairie arrived per plan and set about organizing the kitchen as she envisioned things working. Colly wisely stepped back and gave Cairie a free hand, confident in the knowledge he could tug the reins if need be. The laird and Fiona sat back to watch, firm in their faith of Colly's abilities and Cairie's potential.

The biggest initial change came in the cleanliness of the kitchen and dining areas, which typically was not the biggest focus in pubs. Cairie was adamant that the place become well known for attention to detail. The plates and cups began to sparkle, candles were regularly trimmed and the brass polished, the sand removed and floors scrubbed each morning, rinse water freshly boiled, curtains and napkins laundered, and there was even talk of tablecloths for the weekends. Breads were baked early each day and sandwiches made using fresh meats.

While these details were noticed by the locals—who were drinkers, not eaters, for the most part—travelers began to make regulars stops as word of Cairie's new kitchen made the rounds of her previous customers. She wasn't well known now, although those who did know her were supportive and loyal.

The Hen had taken on something of a new character, not only in the town, but in the region. The local Select Society for Promoting Cooperation, a civic-style organization known for encouraging positive interaction between Roman Catholics and Protestants in North Ayrshire, began holding their monthly meetings there. One

Friday at lunchtime, Colly looked in to find a group of Presbyterian ministers having a lunch of soup and sandwiches with hot tea. He fairly beamed at the progress the Hen had made.

Colly looked resplendent in his role, standing alongside the bar, white apron tied at the waist; he wore dark trousers, a white shirt, a vest, and a tie. His one indulgence was a pair of highly polished hand-fitted shoes which provided comfort during the long hours he spent on his feet.

At the height of each day's meal service, Cairie came out from the kitchen, into the dining room, in her chef's attire: a double-breasted white jacket with black buttons, hound's-tooth pants, and a toque blanche placed jauntily to cover her hair that was wrapped into a bun. Colly thought she overdressed the part a bit, though he understood it made her feel more professional and so he said nothing. She wound her way amongst the customers, inquiring as to their satisfaction. She never returned to the kitchen without going through the bar to speak in a friendly manner to her new customers. The bar food hadn't been forgotten, either. She enhanced the simple fare with spices and sauces, such as to make those partaking of cheaper meals feel special.

The first big challenge for Cairie was the annual Dalry Fall Fair, a highlight of the year for the community; it was a celebration for miners, weavers, farm servants, domestics, and similar workers, and a relief from their monotony and otherwise humdrum lives. Residents looked forward to the sound of music, pipes and drums, some traditional Scottish games of strength, many contests, much dancing, and overall conviviality. No public drinking was allowed; consumption had to be conducted in a licensed facility. Tents were erected by churches and local groups for bake sales, the sale of fresh vegetables and handmade items, and general socializing.

Colly and Cairie arranged for their own tent and offered samples of their food, including several large dishes of haggis provided free of charge—a demonstration of their commitment to the community. And, of course, the Hen did a fabulous business selling beer, stout ales, cider, wines, and a good amount of whisky.

The fair was held during a single weekend, and the reaction of the populace was overwhelming. The Old Speckled Hen's tent became instantly popular. They had made a good business decision; the cost of the food was offset by increased profits from the dining room and bar, and it created tremendous goodwill. Fiona came and greeted old friends in the tent each evening, and the laird sent down his polished carriage to treat wide-eyed youngsters to rides around the village streets. The following Monday the mayor of Dalry, the Blair Mine manager, the millworks superintendent, the priest Father Kelly, and Norman the pastor from the Kilbirnie Auld Kirk Church arrived together at the Hen. They showered Colly and Cairie with thanks from the community. They made clear their desire for The Old Speckled Hen to continue to prosper without impediment. The pair, a bit overwhelmed, realized the Hen had become a community fixture, not merely another business enterprise.

"Your praise will be shared with our partners," said Colly, nervously twisting a napkin in his hands.

And so the legacy of The Old Speckled Hen continued to be burnished.

Colly needed to delicately manage how to exploit the newly found food expertise of the Hen without alienating the base business, who preferred common food and drink. The Scottish people maintained a dislike for those who "put on airs" as it related to times past. They did not approve of landed gentry profiting on the backs of the general populace. Partly due to the personal presence of Colly and his cheerful demeanor, as well as the obvious appeal of Cairie and her joy in making good food, the days of the Hen being a pub focused on the lower classes were in the past. Customers were made to feel welcome regardless of the size of their tab. Other than the variety and quality of the food, most of the changes at the Hen were subtle. The place was so clean it sparkled; gaslights had been installed, making things brighter—although some tables had candles as mood enhancers. The mirror behind the bar, polished weekly, made the bar stand out. Most important, personal warmth and happiness exuded from those who worked there.

One unique addition was the construction of a women's toilet, or loo; it was accessed from inside the pub. It was truly fashionable. Most places had a backhouse near the alley behind the pub, which you reached by taking a side door from the bar area. Backhouses were normally minimally clean, with a kind of privacy partition for the women, and odious, particularly in the summer months. They were chilly in the winter. As more and more women came to enjoy a meal with their spouses, escorts, or friends, it had embarrassed Colly not to be offering more progressive facilities. Off the end of the bar, he installed one of the newfangled ceramic commode closets with a water storage tank several feet above the stool, which one refilled with a hand pump. While some considered it a crude apparatus, it was definitely an attention-getter, in some part due to the loud noise it generated when flushed. People took it in good humor, and it gauged the demonstration of real progress. A pitcher and bowl sat nearby on a small stand, to cleanse one's hands, and a white hand towel was refreshed every so often. The women's loo received less use than the men's, due to the obvious impact of numerous mutchkins of ale and beer served to the lads each day.

Colly took a long-term view about what improved the enterprise, rather than focusing on cost elimination.

"If something is right, it will pay for itself over time, I am sure," became his favorite quote, just after the common, "Thank you for bringing us your business!"

While the Hen developed a reputation for good food, fair prices, excellent service, and a well-kept environment, it was still a pub providing mostly alcoholic beverages to the citizens of a working-class town and, in these times, alcohol was still something of a controversial subject. The "temperance movement," an anti-spirits society, had been founded in nearby Renfrewshire, a county to the north of Ayrshire. It was a follow-on to earlier attempts to promote "moderate drinking." The formalized Moderation Society and Regular Society were outgrowths of these movements which sought to eliminate drunkenness and alcohol abuse in general. Some felt the temperance movement a thinly veiled attempt by industrialists to implement discipline in their workers. The growing involvement of women in social and political issues also influenced the movement. Western Scotland had experienced high immigration numbers of workers from Ireland, with a rising intolerance towards the Irish and Catholics. Mostly, this type of sectarianism affected the larger cities where parades and speeches occurred as firebrands tried to lift the movement at the grass roots. Colly thought the effort well-intentioned, while flying in the face of the role that most established, respectable pubs provided: a place for gatherings and social discourse.

The closest Dalry came to involvement occurred when a carriage of organizers suffered a loose wheel in the middle of town, while on a journey one Saturday to Ayr, in an effort to try and expand the movement. While a local blacksmith worked on reattaching the wheel, some young women from the carriage marched in front of the Hen with signs proclaiming the dangers of alcoholic beverages. Colly stood outside and politely watched, arms folded.

As they climbed back into the carriage, he waved and jovially said, "Many thanks for stopping."

The regulars lifted glasses to his honor when he came back around, behind the bar. But Colly wasn't being cute in his response to the protestors; his parents were, after all, temperance supporters and his manner was always to be pleasant. While privately concerned about the potential effect of the temperance philosophy, he watched the movement cease to become widespread, and life returned to normal.

He did work diligently at maintaining the reputation the Hen had garnered from his efforts. On Saturday afternoons, when the young miners and millworkers, having been paid, crowded the place, it became necessary to keep a watchful eye. At times like these, those inexperienced with consumption could drink at a rate faster than their bodies could absorb the alcohol. No match for these situations physically, Colly used brains—his stock in trade—rather than brawn. And he maintained good relations with some of the more physically intimidating regulars, who knew their assistance might be paid with a free libation when earned. Graeme Keillor, a coal miner, and Roddy Bisset, a mill supervisor, often helped keep the peace, gently escorting disorderly patrons out the door.

Some situations turned tense, as on one rainy Saturday, a busy afternoon with the bar crowded and Cairie getting ready for the evening meal. A young man, not known locally, had too much to drink too quickly and began taking liberties with some of the young staff from country houses nearby.

This offended Colly and he asked the young man to leave, at which the lad suddenly spat out, "Who's making me leave? Not you, you little wanker."

As Colly reached for his elbow to escort him out, the drunk backed away from the bar and the crowd parted, leaving him standing alone.

Colly said, "I'm asking you one more time, nicely, to head out that door and leave my establishment."

The young oaf stood facing the bar, arms down, fists balled, teeth clenched, and face red with rage and embarrassment. "Not until I finish me beer that I paid you for!" he shouted back.

Colly replied, "Sophia, take his beer and give him back his money."

Then Colly reached under the bar and pulled out a club made of wood and lead, wrapped in leather, a common scare piece capable of inflicting pain if necessary. It made a loud thump when he laid it on the bar for everyone to see. He gazed coldly at the young tough, who wisely pocketed some coins the barmaid had placed on the bar, and quickly left. Colly nodded and mouthed a word of thanks as Graeme straightened the stools that had been knocked over. Order was restored in The Old Speckled Hen once again.

Things had reached a high point at the Hen, with the business solid and the restaurant having garnered a regional reputation for quality and value with a varied and creative fare. Most weekends, a line grew in front of the Hen as people queued for a table in the dining room. The concept of taking reservations had not yet developed, although regulars knew to arrive early in order to secure a choice table or one of the limited portions of the special of the day. Cairie had become something of a celebrity and diners were made to feel special when she made one of her now infrequent forays into the dining room. The volume of orders made for a hectic time in the kitchen, which appeared to be in a continual state of change as new methods of cooking were added to accommodate the ever-increasing choices of fine dining.

At least every other month Fiona and the laird dined with Colly and Cairie, fussing over them as they were served a special entree. Colly continued to work hard, taking nothing for granted and avoiding complacency. The Old Speckled Hen had become a roaring success.

And then one Sunday evening, as they were closing the kitchen, Cairie approached Colly and motioned for him to sit.

She removed her toque, shook out the locks of her ginger-red hair, smiled shyly, and said, "I want you to know I have decided to take my leave in two weeks. I am moving to Edinburgh, and you will need a new chef to manage your kitchen. You gave me an opportunity here, and I am truly grateful. I have done what I had hoped to and it is time for me to move on."

Colly was thunderstruck and for a time could only move his lips, unable to form any words. Cleary, Cairie had made her decision, having thought the idea through, so he sighed and nodded.

She continued. "I have a chance to run a private dining room in the prestigious old New Club on Princes Street in Edinburgh. The focus will be on elegant meals, served five nights a week to the members and their guests. In addition, I will be supervising a luncheon service and a team of four other chefs. It is an opportunity I cannot pass."

Since it was not in Colly's nature to feel anger at Cairie's decision, he stood and gave her a warm hug.

"Will you help me in making arrangements for another chef?" he asked hopefully.

"Of course I will," she said. "Be aware I will not be able to stay more than two weeks, under any circumstances."

The next few days were a whirlwind of activity. Colly informed his minority partners of the change, and neither Fiona nor the laird was surprised.

The laird said, "It is the nature of this business for people to do their part and then move on. Don't take it personally."

However, with Colly, everything about the Hen was personal. He still slept every night in the room on the second floor, although it had gradually been improved such that it took on the appearance of a suite in a hotel, with even the office first-rate. In reality, the Hen's staff relationships were business and not familial, but still it bothered him. He was personally invested in running the pub; others saw the work as merely a means of supporting themselves economically.

After a day spent brooding, Colly shook off his sorrow and set about handling the change. The laird again had reached out to his friend Andrew, in Paisley, on Colly's behalf and came away with nothing. Colly realized he should do as planned and discuss Cairie's replacement with her.

"Of course, I have some ideas," she said, and proceeded to share her thoughts with Colly.

A young man on the kitchen staff named Brian Stewart had demonstrated real culinary promise, yet he had not much skill in running and organizing the daily operation. If Colly could step into the kitchen mix to help Brian in the interim, perhaps it might work without interruption. Colly, not sure this was the right move, had always been willing to take a risk when it came to the Hen. He spent day and night with Cairie, documenting the way she prepared the weekly menu, ordered supplies, scheduled staff, cleaned the kitchen, hired and trained staff, and so forth.

As a parting honor, Colly arranged for a daguerreotype photographer to capture an image of Cairie in her double-breasted white jacket, chef's pants, and a starched white toque, henceforth displayed prominently in the dining room of the Hen. Cairie smiled broadly, overwhelmed with the gesture, and Brian saw it with pride for Cairie rather than jealousy.

On her last day, with the luncheon service completed, the entire staff lined the Hen and applauded as Cairie took up the satchel filled with her knives and a couple of personal items. She kissed Colly on his ruddy cheek—which turned him even more crimson—gave a friendly wave, and walked out the door of the Hen and into the carriage the laird had graciously provided. It would carry her to Glasgow to catch the train for Edinburgh. Colly nodded, and everyone went back about their business as usual. Life went on.

Colly realized he had spent some five years building the Hen and the time had passed, seemingly, in the blink of an eye. With no idea what the future held, he knew the fight against complacency had to continue.

Over the years, Fiona McMurdo had maintained her involvement in the pub—but not from a managerial standpoint and not financial, either. Her share of the income, plus the enhanced dividends from Colly, more than provided for her financial needs and comfort; however, they were not a replacement for the missed social interactions with customers, staff, and vendors. Colly understood her needs and accommodated the old woman, enabling her to occasionally "hold court" in the Hen. Now in need of a wheelchair to get around, after several stumbles and falls, Fiona had found a young girl to use the room Cairie had made empty when she left for Edinburgh. In return for free rent, the girl pushed Fiona to the Hen each day after lunch. Colly reserved a table with one chair, exclusively for her use in the afternoons. The wheelchair slid under one end of the table, and the other chair was for whomever Fiona invited to sit with her while she enjoyed a pot of tea. Sometimes she'd ask a favorite customer, or perhaps an employee on a break, or maybe a stranger willing to listen patiently while Fiona regaled them of times past. The one person who almost never sat in the chair was Colly.

"I've heard them old tales many times," he said.

Besides, he didn't have the time. Engaged in virtually every activity associated with the Hen, he was a virtual dervish whirling around the premises. Fiona relished this daily chance to stay engaged with the local populace, who regarded her as a kind of "Queen of the Hen." She never stayed for more than an hour, and the customers who loved her appreciated her presence.

And then one dreary, rainy November afternoon, Fiona didn't appear. Colly couldn't imagine what kept her away from her strict daily routine. He pulled on a coat too long for him due to his size, put a cap on his thinning ginger hair, and walked through the rain two blocks to the flat of rooms where Fiona lived. He rapped his knuckles on the door and waited patiently for it to open. In a moment, the door swung open. Elise, the young woman who functioned as Fiona's helper, welcomed him in with a worried look on her face.

"It is a puzzle," she said. "Fiona claims she is not in the mood to come over to the Hen this afternoon!"

Colly asked if he might speak to Fiona for a moment, and Elise led him to a sitting room with a rug, warming stove, and a table strewn with tea fixings. Fiona sat slumped in her wheelchair.

"Now, Colly," she said, "I'm sorry, I don't feel like conversation today. Please tell my friends at the Hen I might see them tomorrow."

Colly looked into her eyes and said, "My lady, are you ill?"

She smiled tiredly and asked him to please leave her be. Colly held Fiona in high regard and felt further pursuing things to be disrespectful. He took his leave after assuring Fiona he would send a waiter down with a tureen for Fiona and Elise to enjoy as an evening meal. Both of the women smiled enthusiastically at the thought of a fine meal of Brian's soup. And so a hamper was arranged and delivered.

That evening, Colly, exhausted from a long day at the Hen, went to sleep earlier than normal, lulled by the raindrops softly pattering on the slate roof. Suddenly awakened by the sound of someone knocking on the door of his room, he called out to ask who was there. One of the early morning kitchen workers asked him to please come quickly. Colly threw on a shirt and trousers, slipped his feet into a pair of his fitted shoes, and followed the worker down the stairs and into the kitchen. At a table sat a damp and distraught Elise.

"Something's happened to Fiona," she said.

Colly grabbed his coat and followed Elise into the dark, rainy morning and down to Fiona's place. She led him through the flat, to Fiona's bedchamber. Colly feared the worst, and his fears were realized when he saw Fiona had suffered a severe stroke. One side of her body was paralyzed, her face sagged, and she was unable to speak. She recognized Colly, and a tear ran down her cheek as she took her functioning arm and reached for his hand.

Colly firmly grasped the old woman's hand and kept his composure, saying, "Fiona, be comfortable. I am summoning the physician."

A smile crept over the side of her face that still could move, and she shook her head "No," as if to say, "It is my time."

Regardless, Colly sent Elise to fetch the doctor, and sat, holding Fiona's hand tightly.

Young doctor Stuart Mathieson soon arrived at the house with his black bag of medicines and a stethoscope. He looked closely at Fiona and listened to her chest. He then patted her hand and motioned for Colly to follow him out of the room while Elise put a fresh, warm blanket on Fiona.

"Colly," he said, "Fiona has suffered an extreme cerebral hemorrhage, and I do not expect her to survive beyond this morning. Do what you can to keep her comfortable."

He nodded and thanked the doctor, knowing what to do. He asked Elise to brew a pot of tea, and sat down next to Fiona's bed. Occasionally sipping tea, he proceeded to repeat to her the tales of times past which he had heard from her so many hundreds of times. She nodded and smiled and shed some tears. Mostly, she beamed at Colly, who had become something of the child she had never had. And then, after a while, she slipped away.

While Fiona had not been a churchgoer, Colly spoke both to Norman, the Presbyterian pastor from Kilbirnie Auld Kirk Church, and Father Kelly, the Roman Catholic priest. They put together a service of remembrance which the mayor graciously allowed to take place in the city hall for an overflowing crowd. Cairie came from Edinburgh to pay her respects. Mostly locals attended. Hundreds came by to place their hands on the polished casket Colly had purchased for Fiona's body. After the service they walked to the cemetery, where a set of pipes played as she was laid to rest next to her husband, Gordon.

Fiona left all her worldly possessions to Colly: her ownership interest in The Old Speckled Hen, the building which housed her flat of furnished rooms, and a sizable set of deposits in the Bank of Dalry. There were no heirs to contest her wishes—which she had surreptitiously dictated to a barrister only two weeks before, as if she had some sense of foreboding.

Colly absorbed this set of events with his usual sense of aplomb. He assured Elise she could continue to live in her room, rent free, and she began to earn a wage at the Hen as a hostess who welcomed diners and showed them to their tables. He moved Fiona's old wheelchair back under the table where she had "held court" for so many years, and commissioned a local artist to do a colored charcoal sketch of Fiona from memory, to be hung above the table. Friends came by to sit a spell at the table, remembering old times and older tales. They felt Fiona would have liked that.

He went home to Agnes and George, announcing to them they were henceforth retired and could move from their rental into Fiona's flat where Colly could look after them more easily, with Elise's help. Agnes blustered and wept, while George was simply proud that their son was providing for them. It took several weeks to get everything accomplished, and then life went on again as if it always had been that way.

Colly approached his late thirties. In these times in Scotland, he was considered middle-aged. Agnes worried after her son, wishing he had a wife and family. She was, however, secure in the knowledge that Colly was happily wedded to the Hen. His mother was hopeful something eventually would work out between Elise and Colly, but it was not meant to be.

In a short time, Elise, noticed by a young supervisor at the millworks, married and moved out to her own flat with her husband. It thrilled Colly to see her happy and secure. Things were almost perfect, except for what happened to the laird.

The laird was now what could charitably be called "elderly." He still came to his country house in his carriage for most weekends, attended by his aged butler, Fraser. While remaining active managing his many businesses and properties in Glasgow and around Renfrewshire and North Ayrshire, something wasn't quite right with the laird. Colly noticed this when they reviewed the ledgers for The Old Speckled Hen on a quarterly basis. The laird, known for his attention to detail, possessed a keen knowledge of figures going back years, and he had become downright forgetful, struggling with short-term memory. He still dressed formally for dinner each evening, dining alone by candlelight as Fraser served him exquisite dishes prepared by the faithful cook.

Fraser casually mentioned to Colly that the laird had begun to lose his sense of taste, significant for someone who prided himself in his selection of red clarets. Chums from his youth and business associates had begun to die off with regularity, including Andrew, his best friend. The laird began to spend less time in his private clubs in Glasgow and more time in Dalry at the country house. He was particularly saddened by the death of Fiona, his business partner of many years, even though they hadn't been what you could call friends. He had remained personally invested in seeing The Old Speckled Hen survive in order to assure Fiona's well-being.

Fiona was a commoner, the laird an aristocrat. Perhaps that had been the attraction between them. An independent businesswoman in those times was unique. With the passing of each life, the laird became lonelier, exacerbated by his growing enfeeblement. Colly did his best to keep the old codger smiling and engaged when they had their periodic financial reviews of The Old Speckled Hen.

Colly said to him, "Why don't you enjoy some involvement with the community, instead of working constantly?"

"How?" asked the laird, genuinely puzzled at the idea of spending time at endeavors other than business.

"For instance, you could take some of this valuable artwork, hanging here mostly in darkness, and display it in city hall to be enjoyed by the citizens," Colly offered innocently.

"They are mine," said the laird. "Why on earth share them?"

For the first time Colly understood the laird was not like the rest of the people in the community; he considered himself one of the privileged class. The concept of sharing was not something the laird had ever considered. What was his was his and, to his way of thinking, what he had was who he was. The days of peerage and buying loyalty were waning, particularly for individuals like the laird himself, whose social circle drew tighter due to death and infirmity. Colly owed the laird a debt for having taken a chance on him years back, and realized now that the laird had done it for his own interests. Colly tried to see the good in everyone and was dismayed at the laird's loss of sharpness. His diminution made him at risk of being taken advantage of. Colly suspected the bankers and barristers were licking their chops at the sight of the laird's developing weakness. Colly tried to make a point of calling on the laird during his visits to Dalry, offering encouragement and observing the state of things.

Although these days he mostly focused on the business matters of the Hen, Colly still came behind the bar occasionally and helped. He did so, not to take away from the established bartender and barmaids, but rather to stay engaged in the lifeblood of the Hen and with its regular customers. A warm relationship existed between Colly and a few regulars, in that they were aware of each other personally, sometimes with knowledge approaching a level of intimacy.

One, in particular, was Graeme Keillor, a down shaft worker at the Blair Mine located outside of Dalry. An only child of alcoholic parents, Graeme had been orphaned when they succumbed to the ravages of liver disease when he was a boy. Placed in an institution run by a Roman Catholic order, he suffered years of abuse from the nuns and older toughs who took delight in torturing the younger orphans. Graeme was stoic and took the beatings in silence, unwilling to let the tormenters get gratification from his tears. He survived and developed a thick shell which protected him. They turned him out at age twelve—undernourished and psychologically damaged.

Seeking a way through life, he lived on the streets in a kind of feral existence, working jobs where no one else was willing—he cleaned backhouses and mucked stables. Sometimes he stole food and slept in doorways and stables. He developed an even greater hardness and looked at others with a vacant stare. With a strong back and an ability to absorb mind-numbing tasks, he naturally gravitated toward work in the coal mines which dotted the green Scottish countryside southwest of Glasgow. He also developed an unquenchable thirst for alcohol. One surely thought of him as a prime candidate for antisocial behavior, but Graeme never exhibited any outward intolerable deportment.

Graeme began appearing regularly at the Hen, having landed a job as a pumper at Blair. He worked at the bottom of the mine to remove water from the ever-present leaks. His body was hardened by the physical labor, and he was a reliable worker—never tardy despite consuming enormous quantities of alcohol each evening in the illegal shebeens hidden in every alley in the hard-bitten coal towns. Dalry was different; Blair Mines was well respected and did not take advantage of their workers or the towns where their mines operated. Graeme frequented the Hen, drinking two-penny ale by himself, gradually letting inebriation take hold. He quietly left, speaking to no one and causing no problems, only to reappear with the next pay envelope. Colly took notice of him and gave a nod of recognition when serving him a mutchkin of ale.

One day, before serving the ale, Colly took a cloth and wiped the area clean in front of Graeme, saying, "Thank you for your business."

Graeme brightened and smiled, and began to pour forth his story to Colly, seemingly relieved at the chance for pleasant conversation. So began their relationship, with Colly treating Graeme as an equal, as he did every one of his customers. Over time, Graeme became a kind of order enforcer, helping maintain decorum in the Hen. Colly, a realist, recognized the darkness of alcoholism and tried to get Graeme to drink with moderation and eat some healthy food.

Now, getting between an alcoholic and his drinking is a problematic exercise. It resulted in the friendship being sorely tested on occasion, as the downward spiral gradually continued. Colly became encouraged when Graeme unexpectedly courted a young woman from the staff of a local gentry's country house.

Graeme proudly introduced her as the two were sharing an early meal in the Hen. "Colly, this is my Annag."

Colly wiped his hands on his apron and shook her hand, insisting the meal be compliments of the Hen. Annag blushed as Colly warmly shook Graeme's hand, complimenting him on his lovely friend.

When the two were married, Colly generously provided an ample cask of hard cider for the wedding meal. After a while they disappeared, and Colly worried for them, fearful of what Graeme's alcoholism might degenerate into, thinking he should have been able to influence the situation.

Understanding the reality that he had perhaps enabled others with similar afflictions, Colly became more conscious of trying to spot problems. Alcohol is a cultural phenomenon, and he was but a tiny cog in a very large wheel.

Those were turbulent days in the coal and mill country around Ayrshire. An economic recession had threatened the viability of basic industries including weaving and mining. It had a minimal bearing on the profitability of the Hen's business, however, since the cheaper ales and beers which the mill and mine workers consumed were something of a commodity and less profitable. Colly noticed and subtly tightened the belt of the Hen a notch or two, by not filling open job slots and cutting back on higher-end foodstuffs. In doing so, he minimized the encroachment on the cash flow.

He also had strife and disharmony to contend with; both workers and foremen frequented the Hen and this led to some awkward moments. The ownership of the weaving mills had begun to put the squeeze on the workforce by trying to hold down costs while increasing productivity and cutting back hours. These workers mostly lived from one pay envelope to the next, their fears visceral. The loss of income could not be replaced, while rent, food, clothing, and coal still needed to be provided for their families.

Emotions ran high, and there were threats of violence against the mill owners. Colly worried for the town and the workers, reaching out to Father Kelly and Pastor Norman, imploring them to talk of the importance of calm and patience, and arguing at the futility of violence.

Then the unthinkable happened. On the Monday morning shift at the mill, the weavers stayed outside, carrying torches and banners announcing a general strike against the Dalry Woolen Mills. They planned to do no more work until the owners offered formal assurances as to wages and working conditions, and no shipments were allowed in or out. This was made unique by the lack of an existing labor union or even individuals designated to speak for the weavers. Frustration had overcome good logic. Colly spoke, fearful of what the labor unrest might do to the town, as people were taking sides. The miners were concerned about repercussions they might be subjected to if the mill owners reached out to the mine owners.

In general, Colly hoped for harmony, not winners and losers. He fretted when he heard rumors of the mill owners sending for toughs from Glasgow to come down and "break heads" to shut down the strike. After a week with no weakening in the resolve of either party, Colly acted out of desperation for the community and sought out Elise, asking her to set up a clandestine meeting for him with her husband, Robert.

Robert Ogg, one of the youngest foremen at the Dalry Woolen Mills, was perceived to have great potential as a manager. He was not a local boy, having been raised in the Scottish Highlands. He had previously worked for another weaving company owned by the same investors who had founded Dalry Woolen Mills. He possessed a sharp mind with a good head for figures and got along well with people. The position at Dalry, his first supervisory role, was considered a trial which might lead to greater responsibilities.

The secret meeting was to be held at the home of the laird, who for some reason stayed in Glasgow for the week, and Colly received permission to use his study.

When Robert came to the home, Colly greeted him warmly. "How is Elise? I understand she is expecting."

Robert didn't take the bait of friendly talk; he clearly understood Colly had some ulterior motive for their discussion.

He leaned back in one of the leather chairs, crossed his arms over his chest, sighed, and said, "You didn't ask me here to discuss my wife's being with child, now, did you?"

Colly tried to appeal to Robert's good judgement, citing the importance of the woolen mill to the overall health and vigor of the community, and his hope for the parties to end the standoff without violence or economic suffering. Robert listened politely, never uncrossing his arms, as Colly talked about the number of families involved on both sides of the dispute, and asked what concessions from both sides should be considered.

Robert relaxed and said, although he was not authorized to speak for the owners, he thought there was a need for additional efficiencies for the mill to compete with other sites that were becoming less labor intensive. This meant changes in work performance, the acquisition of new skills, and possibly fewer jobs over time. Did Colly think the labor force could consider a change of this magnitude?

Colly sucked on a tooth and thought for a moment. "Are you willing to discreetly discuss this with one of the workers? Not one of the firebrands. Someone more thoughtful. I know them."

Robert thought he could get the ear of the plant manager, who needed to sanction any such effort. Colly promised to speak to a laborer, providing Robert received the encouragement to proceed.

These gentle efforts did lead to nightly meetings, held in secret, over the course of a week in the second-floor office of The Old

Speckled Hen. Colly had prevailed on Gavin MacLeod, a widowed father of four who had been a weaver at the mill for over twenty years, to represent the spirit of the other weavers. Although these discussions were informal, they led to dialogue which made for progress and the eventual settlement of the issues underlying the dispute. Not everyone was happy, yet they were relieved the threat of violence and economic disaster had been averted. Neither Robert, nor Gavin, nor Colly, for that matter, were ever linked to the gentle diplomacy which took place upstairs at the Hen. Sometimes, good citizenship is best when not given recognition. And life went on, pretty much as before.

This turbulence was followed by many years of peace, if not prosperity, for the community of Dalry in general and for The Old Speckled Hen in particular. The pub had a solid reputation as a regional establishment. However, Brian Stewart never enjoyed the culinary success of Cairie Watts. Although competent, he didn't possess the artistic flair of Cairie, in pulling off meals people raved about. His stock in trade was soups and stews, the more pedestrian fare which people loved but would not go out of their way for. Business remained strong, while the rate of growth declined. Not much excited chatter flowed from the dining room. Colly tried to use his imagination to produce a spark to make the Hen vibrant again.

Then, word came that the laird had unexpectedly passed away at his residence in Glasgow. The funeral service happened quickly, involving people from the "city." Colly was not afforded the opportunity to pay respects to the old gentleman who had given him the opportunity of his life. Saddened and not surprised—since the laird had been in serious decline—Colly had never failed to check in with him whenever the laird resided at his country home. Their always warm friendship had been focused almost entirely on their business partnership. There were no heirs, to Colly's knowledge, and he fretted as to the potential effect of the laird's death on The Old Speckled Hen.

Some weeks later, on a Tuesday, a carriage arrived in front of the Hen, and out stepped a young man splendidly dressed in a fine tailored suit, holding an umbrella and a satchel filled with papers. He asked for Colly, who showed the gentleman to the Hen's office so they would have some privacy.

Gerald Dickson removed his hat and introduced himself as a barrister with the Glasgow firm representing the estate of the laird. He explained the laird's holdings were extensive, and no familial heirs existed to whom he could bequeath his wealth. His expertly crafted will left the bulk of his wealth to the Church of Scotland. Norman, the local pastor in Dalry, had bestowed attention to the laird over the years, on behalf of the church, a kindness which the laird appreciated and remembered. Sizable bequests were also made to faithful Fraser and the cook. Monies from the future sale of the country estate were specifically left to the Kilbirnie Auld Kirk, outside Dalry, to fund the needs of the church in perpetuity. The laird had left his interest in The Old Speckled Hen to Colly and, in addition, forgave a sizeable operating loan which the Hen had utilized in lieu of bank loans.

Colly was overwhelmed at the generosity of the laird and his own good fortune as the sole owner of a thriving enterprise—now free from debt in any form. Gerald provided some papers for Colly to sign, to be recorded in the Ayrshire land records and with his firm's trust office. Gerald declined Colly's offer of a celebratory glass of fine Scotch whisky, replaced his hat, climbed into the carriage, and returned to Glasgow.

That evening, Colly went to see George and Agnes with the news of his prosperity. While George smiled with pride, Agnes was fairly bursting with motherly delight over the well-earned good fortune of her Colly.

One spring day soon after, Colly happened to notice Norman, the pastor of Kilbirnie Auld Kirk, finishing a late lunch in the dining room of the Hen, with a gentleman Colly did not recognize. He walked over and extended a hand of friendship to the pastor. Although Colly did not attend services at the church, George and Agnes were longtime members and were fond of Norman, who likewise was fond of the way Colly supported the community.

Norman introduced the other gentleman, a senior figure of the Church of Scotland, down from Glasgow. He referred to Colly as one of Dalry's most prosperous businessmen, which caused Colly to be suspicious of some type of fund drive announcement.

Later the same day, Norman came back by the Hen and explained that he was being considered for a Presbyterian administrative position in the Synod office located in Glasgow, a very prestigious opportunity. The gentleman he had introduced Colly to had come down to gauge Norman's interest in the role, and Norman wanted Colly to be a reference for him. In the community, the promotion was seen as recognition of Norman's kindness, which had resulted in the laird's surprising bequest to the church.

Things worked out for Pastor Norman and, in short order, he relocated to Glasgow. An older gentleman a few years short of retirement replaced him at Kilbirnie Auld Kirk. The church, well-off financially, perhaps needed only a caretaker: someone attentive, not forceful. Pastor Hamish was likable enough, and clearly planned to coast through this ministry.

George and Agnes, alarmed and frustrated, had been close to Pastor Norman for years. Colly tried to give them encouragement. Not a churchgoer, he didn't appreciate their emotions. The old couple began to fade and went out less and less.

One Sunday afternoon Agnes said to Colly, "Your dad and I enjoy each other. We don't need a social life."

For several years, they had a meal each Sunday with Colly, at the Hen. He made sure they were seated away from the drinkers so people didn't think they had become imbibers. Though it was both awkward and humorous, they treasured their time together. George had become thin, and coughed a lot from his years in the mine. Agnes was stooped and somewhat hard of hearing. With Colly, they fairly beamed with pride over what their only child had managed to accomplish.

After the meal, Colly always walked them back to their flat, making sure they were safely inside, checking to see their stoves were banked properly and their coal supply was enough for a few days. Colly found it hard to see them in decline; he always gave

Agnes a big hug and kiss before leaving.

Local wigwaggers whispered as to what was wrong with Colly. Being so prosperous and having no wife and family, perhaps he was a sissy boy. Anytime Agnes and George caught wind of such insults, they loudly took the individuals to task.

In reality, Colly was wedded to The Old Speckled Hen. He considered it more than a job or an investment and dedicated his life to making the Hen a success. His friends and acquaintances were associated with the pub. Colly felt his life fine and lacking for nothing. He held his head high and looked forward to each day.

George went first. One morning, he simply didn't get out of his bed. A neighbor came for Colly, who rushed to his parents' flat and consoled his mother. Death was a rather matter-of-fact thing for Colly. He had experienced the passing of so many of his customers and friends and others; death had kind of numbed him. Not callous by any means, he had feelings, yet always felt the need to stay in control of his emotions. He took care of everything for his dear mother, arranging the undertaker and securing the burial plot plus headstone. He reached out to new Pastor Hamish with George's background, to help with final remarks at the church in case Pastor Norman couldn't make it back. During the service and burial, he held his mother's hand, afterwards walking her back to the Hen, there hosting an after-funeral meal of remembrance. These acts of love fulfilled the role which falls to an only child. Colly offered to sleep in his parents' home for a while so his mother wouldn't be faced with the stress of loneliness. Agnes, emotionally strong, insisted Colly maintain his life while she adjusted to hers.

She managed reasonably well for a few weeks. Agnes took to helping at the new library established in the basement of the city hall and spent most of her mornings there putting books back on shelves, straightening chairs, rearranging newspapers, and showing people how the facility worked. Great therapy, it kept her engaged and amongst people. Every Sunday, rain or shine, she walked with her cane to Kilbirnie Auld Kirk and sat in the same pew space she and George had used since before Colly had been born.

She said to Colly, "It makes me feel close to your father."

This was despite the fact that she didn't much care for the new pastor, whom she thought was just going through the motions at Auld Kirk. It was her church and she was proud of it.

And then one Sunday, she didn't attend. Worried friends rushed to her home after the church services.

She was alone, sitting in a rocking chair near the warm stove, a shawl draped around her shoulders, her worn and dog-eared Bible open in her lap. They found her seemingly lost in thought.

The concerned parishioners sought out Colly, who quickly went to see Agnes, worried over her developing melancholy.

"Son, I'm losing my drive," she told him.

Later in the afternoon, he brought her some of Brian's best soup and a loaf of fresh bread. He banked the stove and tucked her into her bed.

Her eyes shone as she looked at her only child and said, "I love you, son."

"I love you too, Mum," said Colly, with a big smile.

It was the last time they spoke. Agnes passed away in her sleep that night, and Colly found her early the next morning when he went to check on her. Salty tears streamed down his face, and he began the same process completed a few weeks before, for his father. Colly insisted Pastor Norman conduct her service—no harm meant for Pastor Hamish, just how Agnes wanted it. Her body was interred in the cemetery, next to George's, the earth still fresh on his grave. Those present suspected George was there waiting, his hand held out for her. As Colly thanked people for coming, shaking hands around, he felt true loneliness for the first time in his life.

In Scotland in the mid-nineteenth century, as well as most of the rest of the world, conventional wisdom said trouble comes in threes. Or fours! Or fives, or whatever number we use to rationalize away bad things which happen in life.

A scant four weeks after his mother's death, Colly awakened with a sense of foreboding. Something wasn't right. Sitting up in bed, he listened closely. A low sound, kind of like thunder from a long way off, came from somewhere. He put on his pants and shoes, grabbed his robe, and went down the steps, into the darkened Hen. It was not totally dark—a strong glow was coming in the windows. He opened the door of the pub, horrified to see high flames engulfing the tenement down the street where his parents had lived, in Fiona's old flat. Colly had not even completed removing his mother and father's possessions from the flat. He ran down the narrow street toward the flames, unsure of how he could help.

The town's fire wagon was there, and volunteers manned the hand pumps which put forth a pitiful stream of water to flow onto the structure. Colly noticed the wind and wasn't sure whether it came from weather or from the hungry fire sucking oxygen into itself.

Grayson, the lead firefighter for the town, shouted instructions to wet down the surrounding buildings. "Get them wet, boys, before we lose control of her!"

Colly realized the whole town could burn if they didn't take quick action. He directed some bystanders to follow him as he ran to the back of the Hen, grabbing a stack of pails. They arranged a kind of bucket brigade as he pulled over a ladder and proceeded to begin dumping buckets of water onto the thatched roof portion of The Old Speckled Hen, not worried about the slate roof portion which the sparks shouldn't ignite. When the thatching had been thoroughly soaked, they moved to the next building's roof closer to the fire, also a thatch. And so it went, the battle for survival enjoined until they came so close to the fire the heat of it repelled them.

By now, the tide had turned. The tenement building Colly owned was a complete loss, its roof caved in and walls teetering on collapse. The buildings on either side were damaged, yet still standing. Looking around, one could easily see the whole of the town had been engaged to avert the disaster: miners, weavers, shopkeepers, wives, mothers, even older children. Everyone had done their part. Community meant something to them. The kitchen crew of the Hen had come to work, and Colly put them to preparing sandwiches and coffee, which were freely distributed amongst the crowd of volunteers.

The next few days were spent cleaning the destruction, with talk of rebuilding and repair. Colly shook off the financial loss of the building; he had some rudimentary insurance coverage from the Glasgow risk pools. While still emotionally impaired over the loss of his parents, he was not going to let his priorities get off-kilter over something as inconsequential as money.

A couple of weeks later, he threw a fundraiser at the Hen to raise money to help those displaced by the fire, for a time adding meals from the Hen to the fund. Both the mill and the mine kicked in some monies, and Kilbirnie Auld Kirk made an appeal to collect household items and clothing. In time, things sorted out for those affected by the fire. And then life went on, pretty much as before.

As a business enterprise, The Old Speckled Hen was virtually indefatigable: open daily and serving mostly common food and drink to a vast and fiercely loyal customer base. The staff was very experienced, honest, skilled, and proud to be associated with what had become a regional institution again. This attitude of the workers gave the Hen its personality.

Then another shoe fell, and the resiliency of the Hen became sorely tested. During the second week of January, people in the town of Dalry were emotionally over the positive peak which encompasses Christmas and Twelfth Night. About eleven o'clock on Tuesday morning, the sound of the steam whistle at the Blair Mine trilled mournfully across the countryside, alongside smoke billowing out of the shaft and through the topside gantry, where the rescue bell clanged wildly. It appeared some type of explosion or fire was coming from underground.

A strong team of four horses pulled the red fire wagon swiftly up the hill, from the town to the mine. Townspeople swarmed to the mine, anxious for word about their loved ones and friends. Guards at the mine tried to keep order, and the mine superintendent fought to get accurate information amidst the confusion. Mining families still remembered the Nitshill Mine disaster in Renfrewshire the year before, which took the lives of sixty-one miners and maimed dozens of others. The Blair explosion had caused a temporary loss of steam pressure throughout the site and the cages had to be winched to the surface by hand.

A murmur went through the crowd when the first cage reached the surface and a dozen miners limped off the cage, into the arms of rescue personnel and other workers. They were black with grime and soot as to be mostly unrecognizable. Still ambulatory, a few of them knelt and kissed the surface of the earth, thankful to be safely above ground. In reality they were coal miners; down the mine shaft was where they added their value, and they soon would return to the depths to gouge at the seams of the soft coal. They were rushed away from the cage, which needed to be lowered in order to get to those still below, both injured and dead. This group had been en route topside when the calamity occurred. The blast from the explosion and resulting fire rushed up the shaft and made it hard to breathe.

As the cage began to disgorge its loads from below, it became apparent there had been a significant loss of life. The mine staff erected some large tents off to the side where the wounded or dead were taken for either triage or identification. Supervisors were seen coming from the tents to call for specific families, who were taken to see their loved ones.

Colly stood helpless and off to the side, seemingly overwhelmed by another tragedy. Then he shook his shoulders and began to help Father Kelly and Pastor Hamish minister to the families who had lost their husbands, fathers, brothers, and uncles.

The sorrow was indiscriminate and widespread, with screams, howls, and keening filling the air as emotions exceeded the breaking point. Colly's knack for being able to calm and comfort people in emotional pain—a kind of gift he had never been aware of—had him tending to the grieving. His sort of detachment, from years of trifling interactions at the Hen, proved valuable since people became emotionally vulnerable when alcohol released facile inhibitions. Now it came in handy; he was able to absorb people's deepest, heart-rending expressions of grief. He held hands, gave hugs, and otherwise provided comfort. He dispatched others to the Hen to bring out great jugs of coffee and warm rounds of bread, fresh from the oven. Sustenance provided solace. Once again, Colly and the Hen were there for the townspeople.

The officials at Blair's determined there were nine miners dead and several more injured. It took many months before the emotional wounds began to heal. It was part of life in these Ayrshire towns; tragedy was not uncommon.

The beginning of the last half of the nineteenth century was a cathartic time for southwest Scotland, with the economic crisis and continued mechanization placing a great deal of pressure on business and industry, particularly in the mining and weaving communities. There were no new jobs for young people or those with only their goodwill and physical strength as marketable skills. The change started gradually, with young people leaving for the larger cities, particularly those with ports where shipping companies provided some opportunities. By the 1870s, it had become a virtual Scottish exodus for those looking to establish productive lives in England or, more often, the United States. Those with experience or at least some knowledge in coal mining or textiles could hope for a good prospect at employment, as those industries were still burgeoning in the relatively new nation.

Regular customers of the Hen sought out Colly, hoping he could advise their children not to join their brethren in the search for a good life. While Colly could be deemed a trusted advisor, he wasn't a magician. They came to him and pleaded for him to lend an ear to the plight of their Raymond, or Seamus, Duncan or Jack, James or Lewis, or Charles. The name didn't matter … the plight was the same. In their late teens, they were always strong and very bright, according to the parent, but with no special skills and limited experience save the odd job at the mine or the mill. With the girls, the same applied: always beautiful, looking for something local, to be around to care for the parents who, in coming old age, soon needed them. The girls were offered not much hope, what with the decline in housing staffs amongst the gentry who had begun to simplify their homes and households due to the trying economic times. Ultimately, the girls followed the boys wherever they flocked, to have some hope of a matrimonial chance.

Colly learned to be polite and frank regarding the limited local opportunities for the coming generation of workers. Although there were no assurances, leaving for the United States offered a better opportunity for those with limited skills. So they crossed the Atlantic with, literally, the clothes on their backs, and perhaps a name of someone who had found work in textiles or coal.

Many an acquaintance became bitter at Colly for his candor. Old Gavin MacLeod, who had helped Colly settle the mill's labor trouble those years before, felt Colly owed him and should develop an argument as to why his children should stay in Dalry. Colly, the voice of reason, said times had changed, and the youth had to make hard decisions for themselves, as the youth had for many generations. Gavin's lips tightened. He nodded to Colly, finished his beer, and never darkened the door of The Old Speckled Hen again.

Colly took these actions by others very personally, however misguided they may have been. He had never asked to be thrust into the role of arbiter of people's lives. A good, kind, generous man, he knew no other way to respond to life's challenges than by being honest. This exodus of the youth had a depressive effect on Colly. This, combined with the loss of his parents, Fiona, and the laird, the devastation of the fire and mine disaster, and the strike at the mill, he had had enough of what he was willing to stand. He felt it time for a major change in his life. He had turned fifty, and the years of toil at The Old Speckled Hen had taken their toll. For the first time in his life he had a total feeling of emptiness, as if he had used up his ration of life.

He had maintained an informal relationship with Gerald Dickson, the Glasgow barrister who had represented the laird's estate. Colly seldom had a real need for legal services, though he thought it good for a businessman of his stature to have a professional contact in Glasgow, the industrial and financial hub of southwest Scotland. In the lull of late winter, when one thinks spring will surely never arrive, he sent word to Gerald, asking for a meeting to discuss a commercial matter.

When the appointed day came close, Colly placed the Hen under the responsibility of his most trusted employee, Glenn, and took his leave. He was "just taking a few days of rest in the city to brighten my life," a story most people were happy with, although it was the most un-Colly-like thing they had ever heard. He boarded a coach which took him through the countryside and to the bustling city of Glasgow, with its tall buildings and many church spires, lots of coal smoke flowing from chimneys, and people everywhere.

Gerald had graciously made arrangements for Colly to lodge in the stately Queen Street Hotel, a legendary place where people of means stayed. Nothing about Colly spoke of ostentatiousness, so he might have been uncomfortable in the Queen. A diminutive man, very well dressed and carrying a simple valise, he strode up the stairs and into the polished lobby of the grand hotel. He paused at the registration desk, gave his name, and insisted he wanted a modest room, regardless of what Mr. Dickson may have arranged. A bellman escorted Colly to the third floor, where he placed a key in a room door which opened into a lovely bedchamber, with carpeting covering the whole floor and a radiator for the newfangled steam heat beneath the sole window in the room. A large bed faced the window and a table with two chairs. A closet with running water, a tub, and a commode completed the suite. The bellman hesitated, and Colly realized the man was waiting for a gratuity, which Colly provided—unsure of the proper amount. When the bellman exhibited a warm smile, this told Colly he had overachieved. He chuckled to himself over his naivety and thrift. He laid open the valise on a couch at the end of the bed, placed a chair by the window, parted the curtains, and sat, surveying the scene below.

Glasgow in the 1870s was a city past the peak of its glory. The economic recession had hurt it and, although he saw a bustle of activity, it was clearly in decline. Not as many smokestacks spewed forth yellow-tinged coal smoke, nor were the streets clogged with drayage. Still, it was a rather busy scene of a city that was content with itself. The weather felt cold and damp, with a hint of coming snow. Colly caught himself nodding off, the victim of travel weariness.

When night fell, he arose from the chair and went to a sink alongside the tub, and splashed cold water on his face in an attempt to freshen. In a looking glass over the sink, he was surprised to see his graying locks and sallow cheeks. He still felt good for his age, but time waits for no man.

He went down to the main floor, to be seated by a waiter in the dining room, off to the side at a table for two. He looked around and observed the diners: couples, husbands and wives, plus one or two other single men. He ordered some bread, a meat pie with vegetables, and a glass of claret—a rarity for him. He ate slowly, savoring the food and the atmosphere. This was a momentous trip for him. Back in his room, he found that a chambermaid had turned down the bedclothes, and he undressed. His body fairly sighed as he slipped under the comforter.

Colly awakened early the next morning to the muffled sound of horses' hooves clopping against the cobblestone streets as they pulled milk delivery wagons; this was much more noise than he ever experienced in the heart of Dalry. He freshened and dressed, repairing to the dining room for a breakfast of toast, jam, porridge, and hot tea. Back at the room, he left things for the maid to straighten.

Excited but anxious over his coming business discussion, Colly walked down the polished stairs to the lobby. He left his key with the desk clerk, borrowed an umbrella, and proceeded down the street to the offices of Gerald Dickson's law firm. Greeted at the entryway of the firm and shown into a room with a long, library-style table, he saw Gerald, one of his partners, and a middle-aged woman who appeared to be a stenographer. Colly sat at one table end, and after a few pleasantries, got right to the heart of the discussion.

After more than thirty years of running The Old Speckled Hen, he felt the need to consider passing ownership to another individual or partnership or firm. He had built a very solid business, but was mentally exhausted and physically not the man he used to be. He laid out papers detailing revenues, expenses, assets, a breakdown of growth and declines, quarterly regulatory filings as required by the Crown, employee data, even copies of the current dining and beverage menus.

Gerald, pleased with the amount and level of detail, asked if Colly had a potential buyer in mind. Smiling, Colly responded that for years he had been hoping to entice Cairie Watts to return from Edinburgh and take over ownership of the Hen. Alas, on inquiry, he discovered Cairie had married a prominent gentleman member of Edinburgh's New Club some two years before and had moved with him to London. Her husband had opened a new office for his firm and they had taken in a child as their own and were raising her in London. Cairie had always managed her priorities properly and running an independent business paled in comparison to her other opportunities.

Colly told Gerald, "I should be pleased if you could identify an individual seeking a challenge, with a head for figures, who is also personable and caring, and interested in making a difference in a community."

Gerald and his partner seemed befuddled; they were accustomed to straightforward transactions and impersonal, unemotional business arrangements. The stenographer smiled brightly, seemingly thrilled to have come across a Scotsman who saw life in terms other than pounds and shillings. The partners excused themselves to another room while the stenographer, named Willa, and Colly chatted. They happily shared a pot of tea and some biscuits which an attendant brought into the room.

Gerald returned by himself, coughed into his hand, and said, "The firm will be pleased to accept this engagement under our normal terms of compensation, plus any usual and reasonable expenses. We will dictate something to Willa, who will take it to your hotel for your signature, if the terms are acceptable to you. This will enable you to return to Dalry on the morning coach."

The process of selling The Old Speckled Hen had begun.

Colly, somewhat bewildered at what he had unleashed that afternoon, wandered the city for a while, breathing in the sights, sounds, and smells. He bought a crumpet and nibbled at it on a park bench, too nervous for a proper lunch. At midafternoon, he returned to his hotel room and washed his hands and face in the bowl. While he dried with a towel, there came a knock on his door. A bellman advised he had a lady caller waiting for him in the lobby. He put his jacket back on, checked to be sure his shoes were properly polished, and ran a comb through his thinning hair.

He strode to a table in the lobby and greeted Willa Cather, who stretched out her hand. She had a satchel of documents, pen and ink, and a blotter. As she explained the content of the agreement, she shyly watched Colly, who was mesmerized by the whole affair. He signed the papers with a flourish and then brashly asked Willa if she could join him for tea. She was embarrassed, although it was the end of the day and she was not expected to return to the barristers' offices until the next morning.

While she worried about the propriety of a personal engagement with a client, her enthusiasm got the better of her concerns. They had a delightful conversation about Glasgow, the weather, their personal interests (he had none, save the Hen), music, and food. They laughed and smiled the whole while. As night fell, she stood and excused herself, saying she had an elderly father to attend to. She gave Colly a hug and walked out into the night.

Colly was overwhelmed at having had a warm, personal conversation with an attractive woman who had no agenda and wanted nothing from him other than pleasant conversation. He thought, perhaps, he might be capable of romantic feelings.

The next morning he checked out of the hotel, having been instructed by Gerald to bill it to the firm. His trip back to Dalry passed uneventfully, yet seemingly it was not the same place he had left. Decisions he had already made changed the course of his life significantly—not that his grasp of the Hen became any less; he simply had decided to take his life in a different direction.

In the coming days there were no rumors about the Hen, only observations to the effect of something different about Colly. He embodied more of a detachment, if you will. A fortnight passed, and another, and then a dispatch arrived, summoning Colly for another meeting with Gerald in Glasgow. Again, Colly asked Glenn to watch over the Hen, and booked a coach seat for the trip.

The stay at the Queen Street Hotel was now taken for granted. In the morning, after breakfasting, he walked to the barristers' offices. Filled with anticipation, he was ushered into the very same conference room to meet with Gerald. The firm had identified a young man meeting the criteria Colly had established in their prior meeting, someone who clerked in a business with relations with the firm. Gerald had known the business owner for some time, and the man vouched for the candidate as if he were his own son. While the young man had limited funds, Gerald said the business owner and his friends would stand the young man to a substantial down payment if an arrangement could be worked out for some type of "earn out" over time. In other words, could an agreement be crafted in which Colly shared some of the risks? Colly cocked his head and thought to himself for a while. He wanted to make a clean break from the Hen, fearful of any future involvement leading him back into the midst of managing the property. However, he reminded himself that the laird had taken a chance on him lo those many years ago.

Colly suggested a discussion among the three parties to determine whether there existed enough compatibility. "I am hopeful something could be arranged on the morrow."

As the meeting ended, Gerald smiled shyly and knowingly, offering regrets to Colly from Willa, who was off on a bit of leave to care for her father, who had taken a turn for the worse. Colly blushed and thanked Gerald for the discreet comment.

Against his better judgement, the same evening Colly had the hotel dining room prepare a hamper of special foods and cakes, with a jeroboam of fine white wine. He arranged for a bellman to hand deliver them to the address Gerald had provided. Willa, and maybe her father, would enjoy a surprise, delightful evening repast, courtesy of Colly.

The next morning, in the barristers' offices again, William Collins was introduced to Harry Bailey and his patron, Robert Livingston. Gerald had arranged the meeting in his personal office for the three of them to get acquainted. Harry, in his early twenties, was thin, of normal height, with ginger hair and ruddy cheeks. Soft-spoken and earnest, he exuded self-confidence. The youngest child of parents in poor health, he had finished school and taken a job in Livingston's company, doing accounts. Unmarried, he said he knew the value of hard work.

"How so?" asked Colly.

"I paid for my keep in school by shoveling coal into basement chutes for two pence per ton." Harry spoke evenly, not boastful, simply matter-of-fact.

Robert attested to the long hours Harry had willingly worked as he tried to gain experience. The more they talked, the more relaxed Colly became. He inquired of Robert as to whether the earnest loan was to be secured by an interest in the Hen.

"No," responded Robert, "it is secured by our interest in Harry."

This comment was enough for Colly. He instructed Gerald to write instruments he and Robert thought fair, based on the provided financials. Colly shook hands around and prepared to take his leave.

Gerald took Colly aside and gave him an envelope which smelled of lilac. In his coach, he opened the note of thanks from Willa, for the hamper of food and wine which had brightened her spirits and her father's. She expressed a strong desire to see him again. Colly felt emotions he had never experienced. In a few days, when he received the papers from Gerald, the terms were generous and predicated on an approval visit from Harry. Colly executed the documents, handing them back to the courier, along with a note inviting Willa to dinner during his coming visit to Glasgow.

Some two weeks later, for the first time, Harry Bailey visited The Old Speckled Hen. As Colly toured him about, Harry asked many thoughtful questions, taking no notes, as if he was filing the information in his head, much like Colly had done his whole life. Colly anticipated the questions, including the one about where Colly planned to reside.

Some years before, he had rebuilt the tenement building which had been destroyed by fire, and it contained several apartments. But Colly felt living close by to be a distraction for them both and detract from Harry's leadership and role in the community. Instead, having been appointed a director of the advisory board of Robert Livingston's company, Colly planned to engage temporary lodgings in Glasgow. Who knew for sure what direction the remainder of his life might take, particularly if the romance with Willa blossomed?

They agreed to announce the purchase of The Old Speckled Hen by Harry Bailey and his partners, by displaying a legal notice in the city hall. In this manner, others learned of the transaction at the same time and with the same information, leaving no room for rumors or gossip. The morning the sale was posted, Harry and Colly had a meeting at the Hen for the employees. Many were relieved, as a change had been expected due to Colly's subtle behavioral shifts.

On a Saturday, Colly hosted a farewell and an opportunity to meet Harry, to be attended by the longstanding, faithful customers of The Old Speckled Hen. Colly endured many tears, handshakes, and hugs from those who truly loved him. He beamed throughout, wishing George and Agnes could have been there to witness his celebration.

The next day, the party long over and the Hen cleaned, Colly took a last, long amble around the place, gazing at the tables and chairs as he had thousands of times, making sure everything was in order. He had forgotten how dim the place could be on a late winter afternoon. The stove was putting out some heat, the smell of the burning coal a familiar faint perfume to his nostrils. He straightened a few chairs and checked the salt shakers. He looked at the walls; gaslights were turned down, so the shadows had disappeared. The stools at the bar were empty. He took a damp cloth and wiped the wood down, its smooth surface dimpled with scratches and a few, very few, burn marks. Looking at his own reflection in the mirror, he wondered where the time had gone. He reached into his pocket and took out the set of keys, placing them in Harry's outstretched hand.

He smiled and wished Harry good luck. Then William Collins walked out the door of The Old Speckled Hen and into the gloaming.

# GIRL FROM THE NORTH COUNTRY

When Garrick McCaig unexpectedly succumbed to a stroke at age forty, in 1870, it devastated Cairie Watts McCaig. Unfamiliar with London, she resided there with her husband a scant eight months, still adjusting to the role of serving as mother to Jesse, the orphan girl she and Garrick had taken in. Garrick's firm had been kind and supportive during the aftermath of his tragic attack, prepared to relocate Cairie and Jesse back to Edinburgh, the firm's base. Maybe out of insecurity, or more likely out of fear, Cairie decided to return with her daughter to the safety and comfort of the North Country from which she had made exodus more than two decades previously. And so they did.

Cairstine "Cairie" Watts grew up in the seaside Highlands of western Scotland, in the Argyll and Bute region of Strathclyde. Cairie was the child of a single mother—the widow of a military man—who had raised a daughter by herself. Ma Watts didn't talk much about her late husband to Cairie, or to any others, for that matter. He hadn't been around much … barely long enough to father a child. Ma figured it as part of the past and not helpful to the present. It made for a spartan childhood for Cairie, on a tiny soldier's pension; however, it sufficed. Mother-daughter relationships are often troublesome, yet theirs was warm and loving, helped along by their having only each other. Cairie did her part by being a good daughter, minding both the rules and her tongue.

The place, called Cladich, more a village than a town with some houses, a post office, an inn, and a school, spread out along the road to Inveraray. Farmhouses with brilliant green grass and flocks of sheep dotted most of the surrounding rolling hills. It was called picturesque when the sun shone, which was seldom—what with storms and rain rolling in from the west, off the Irish Sea. The thatched cottage they lived in had been passed down from Ma Watts's aunt and had been in the family for several generations. Sturdy and dry, with a fireplace fueled with peat cut from a moor down the road, near Creag Bracha, it had been around as long as anyone could remember. The fire burned smoky and fragrant, and warded off the damp chill nicely, casting a soft glow around the main room. Oil lamps provided the real light, plus the extravagance of a glass window in the south-facing wall. Cairie and Ma shared a room, each with their own bed warmed by stones from the fire in the wintertime.

The local school provided Cairie the socialization she needed while learning her letters and figures. Children from around the area farms came to study with the young teacher who lived in a room at the inn. The dark months were for school, since summer provided long days with barely more than a twilight at night. Ma stayed involved in her daughter's life as much as any single parent of an only child could. The pension income provided basic needs but no luxuries, the same situation as the other kids in the school. Cairie took her studies seriously, realizing that education provided a potential means for improving her life.

By her early teens, she was what you could call a classic comely Scottish lass, of medium height and build, with long locks of ginger hair and rosy cheeks. Cairie brought along a smile which warmed you. Popular among the others, she had demonstrated an interest in, and talent for, cooking. Ma Watts, not what one would think of as an accomplished cook, having been raised with simple stews and warm, coarse bread, and seldom serving a crisp salad, took no interest in trying new things or maintaining a kitchen garden as did some of her friends and acquaintances. Cairie began reaching out to the women in the village and on surrounding farms, trying to learn their favorite methods of preparing and serving food. Over time, she became proficient in cooking common meals in ways which made them appear unique and tasty. When community meals were put on at fairs and church socials, Cairie's contributions were sought out and quickly consumed.

In a part of Scotland where culinary expertise rarely stood out, Cairie commanded attention. She began getting opportunities in what today might be called "catering," providing complete meals for weddings, wakes, church events, and government meetings. Cairie, ill-prepared to provide volumes of food, had limited facilities for cooking, and Ma Watts provided not much help, clearly in awe of her daughter's talents. Granted frequent use of the kitchen in the basement of the local Church of Scotland, Cairie saw it as a rudimentary beginning. It allowed more space and countertops for the prep work she perceived as the key to good food. Within a year she had outgrown the church kitchen and knew she needed to step into a more formal role. With the support and encouragement of Ma Watts, Cairie managed to find an entry role as a kitchen assistant in a restaurant in Dumbarton, many miles to the southeast from Cladich, in fact a day's journey.

The opportunity came about, strangely enough, through the pastor of the local church who had friends in Dumbarton. They had heard the raves regarding this new food favorite from Cladich. One thing led to another and Cairie got the chance, based solely on her reputation.

As she left, there were no tears and Ma told her daughter she "was proud for and of her."

Promised the use of a room furnished by the pastor's friends and with the confidence of youth, Cairie made the journey for her first big chance in life, carrying a valise containing clothes lovingly created by Ma Watts, and not much else. It was clearly entry-level work, yet a professional chance nonetheless, offering long hours and real experience from a seasoned staff. Cairie did everything, from washing dishes to provisioning prep tables, even sometimes serving as a member of the waitstaff. She absorbed it all—filled with her hunger for knowledge and experience. Her attitude and pleasant manner set her apart. A quick study, she gained notice and was soon awarded with opportunity.

When the chief cook took the chance to move to a bigger restaurant in Glasgow, Cairie and two others of the staff were invited along. Now in her late teens, she saw this as a means of expanding her experience. She did not consider it in a romantic sense; rather, she had a desirable skillset which made her unique and quested after. The city restaurant had a clientele much more discerning and demanding. Underfunded, unfortunately, and despite her hard work, the place closed within a year, yielding her not much more than an expanded set of skills. Cairie continued to impress, and moved to another established place in the city, in a role more focused to honing her culinary skills. She became talented in what were known as "starters" and salads, plates which established flavors and textures, thereby enhancing the main courses. Not quite an artist yet, Cairie nevertheless demonstrated creativity, which impressed the diners.

Andrew, a prominent businessman and regular customer, well connected in Glasgow's upper crust, and some partners were interested in starting a restaurant in Paisley, a town to the west of Glasgow where a number of city dwellers maintained country homes. These individuals had expectations for prepared food which exceeded the fare provided by the existing restaurant trade, and Andrew and his fellow investors intended to exploit the opportunity. They approached the chef and inquired as to whether he could assemble a team to start an enterprise focused on serving quality food. Wary of another situation with financial pressures, the chef demurred … until reassured by the partners that this chance stood to satisfy real culinary expectations. As the chef approached his team, Cairie particularly understood the risks and opportunity, in addition to a realization of the wandering nature of a career in fine dining.

Having turned twenty and on the cusp of culinary recognition, she didn't think twice before telling the chef, "I am glad for the chance."

While Andrew and the partners may have been established gourmands, they were, first and foremost, businessmen. They understood the chef may run the kitchen and turn out meals which were impressive in their taste and presentation; however, if it could not be done profitably, the enterprise failed. Pricing and portion controls were new concepts to the emerging fine dining trade, along with the realization there were individuals willing to pay for subtle differences in gustatorial talent which differentiated between fine dining and trenchermen consumption. The lessons were eye opening for aspiring artists like Cairie, yet she possessed a sharp wit, listening intently during the periodic business reviews the partners required and which she was privileged to attend. Working through a continuing struggle, the teams coalesced and within four years the restaurant became well established and attracted additional customers from within Glasgow city proper.

Things weren't perfect. Cairie worked long hours and had virtually no social life outside of the restaurant. And while she had honed her talents, most of the credit and acclaim accrued, quite rightly, to the chef, who also functioned as a quasi–general manager. The chef understood this and had quietly mentioned to the partners about potential burnout of their employees. Andrew sniffed and said something to the effect that "team management is not my responsibility." Not altogether coldhearted, he filed the comment away for future use. Some weeks later, Andrew shared a drink in his private club on Queen Street in Glasgow, with one of his best friends, a chap he had known since they were boarding school chums years ago. The individual, a landowning laird of some note in Glasgow social circles, extremely well regarded, and one of the few individuals whom Andrew referred to as a close friend. Friendships were a rare thing among the upper classes in Glasgow, something closely managed and nuanced, not taken lightly. The laird had a difficult business situation and reached out to Andrew for advice.

Knowing it was a serious matter, Andrew called for a waiter to freshen their fine mellow whiskies. It appeared the laird had made an investment in a good-sized pub in Dalry, to the south—an enterprise on the cusp of growth—and had taken on a new partner-manager some time before. The individual wanted to expand the enterprise into something of a regional food presence. To do so they needed a first-class chef or at least someone aspiring to be so. The laird knew Andrew as a managing investor in a fine dining place in Paisley, who perhaps knew of a potential candidate. Andrew lifted his crystal drink glass and examined the caramel-brown liquor against the candlelight as he thought for a moment.

"Perhaps I have an idea," said Andrew to the laird. "May I get back to you in two weeks?"

The laird nodded appreciatively, knowing a favor asked and granted created an obligation.

Andrew sought out the chef the next week and explained the situation. "Perhaps we can solve two problems," said Andrew.

The chef broached the matter with Cairie, flattered although not overly excited. "A pub," said Cairie, "not exactly something to be hoping for as a next step."

The chef presented this as an opportunity to demonstrate talent independently and develop as a manager, chances which were rare. And if Andrew endorsed the situation, probably of minimal risk. The chef told her she had a couple of days to think about things before they considered other individuals. The next morning, Cairie told the chef she at least wanted to explore the possibility, if he might kindly communicate her interest. Andrew immediately sent a telegraph to the laird in Glasgow, suggesting a meeting in Dalry with the principals.

The small population of Dalry made Cairie uncomfortable. Even so, out of respect for Andrew she agreed to attend the meeting. The laird and his primary partner, William Collins, or "Colly" for short, were a bit taken aback on meeting her, as they had expected a male candidate rather than female.

Colly patiently listened to her concerns, and then proceeded to share with Cairie his dream of turning the pub into something of an area food destination and a "must stop" for travelers on their way to or from the southern coast of Scotland. He described the investment that had been made in the facilities and his ideas for developing a menu. Cairie listened politely and, finally, the laird suggested a carriage ride to view The Old Speckled Hen.

Colly proudly trekked Cairie through the pub, his enthusiasm infectious. She folded her arms and asked some questions, particularly about potential suppliers of foodstuffs, meat, milk, vegetables, and so forth. The pub, not as small as she had thought and not as large as she had hoped for, did have potential. Colly voiced concerns that the current kitchen staff not feel threatened since they had been loyal, yet affirmed Cairie had charge of managing the kitchen.

The laird nodded to Colly, who swiftly made Cairie an offer of employment. Aware that chances like this didn't often come along, Cairie didn't hesitate and they struck an agreement.

The process of extricating herself from the restaurant in Paisley took Cairie a couple of weeks. During this time Colly discussed the change with the kitchen staff of the Hen, who reacted positively since the commitments the owners were making provided hope for a solid future. Fiona McMurdo, the original owner of the Hen, stepped forward and made an offer to Cairie, for the use of a room in her nearby flat, to ease into the community, which made the local transition quick and seamless.

Cairie arrived per plan and set about organizing the kitchen as she envisioned things working. Colly wisely stepped back and allowed Cairie a free hand, confident in the knowledge he could tug the reins if need be. The laird and Fiona sat back to watch, firm in their faith of Colly's abilities and Cairie's potential.

The biggest initial change came in the cleanliness of the kitchen and dining areas—typically not the biggest focus in pubs—and Cairie was adamant that the place become known for attention to details. The plates and cups shined, candles were regularly trimmed and the brass polished, floors were scrubbed each morning, rinse water boiled for dishes, curtains and napkins laundered, and even talk of tablecloths on the weekends. Breads were baked in the ovens each day and sandwiches made from fresh meats. The locals, who were drinkers and not eaters, for the most part, noticed this, and travelers began to make regular stops as word of Cairie's new kitchen made the rounds.

In no time, the Hen became known as "the pub with the chef." The community didn't quite know what to make of their flamboyant new resident. At the height of each day's meal service, Cairie came out from the kitchen, into the dining room, in her chef's attire, a double-breasted white jacket with black buttons, hound's-tooth pants, and a toque blanche placed jauntily to cover her ginger hair wrapped in a bun. Some thought she overdressed the part a bit, while understanding it made her feel more professional. Cairie wound her way amongst the tables of customers, inquiring as to their satisfaction, and she never returned to the kitchen without going through the bar in a friendly manner, building potential future customers. The bar food wasn't forgotten by her, either, with the simple fare served there enhanced with spices and sauces such as to make those partaking of cheaper meals feel special.

The annual Dalry Fall Fair soon came along, always a highlight of the year for the community: a celebration for miners, weavers, farm servants, domestics, and so forth—a relief from their monotony and otherwise humdrum lives. It was very lively, with the sound of music, pipes and drums, some traditional Scottish games of strength, many contests, much dancing, and overall conviviality. Churches and local groups erected tents for bake sales, fresh vegetables, handmade items, and general socializing. The Hen arranged for its own tent, which offered free samples of food and several large dishes of haggis, a demonstration of commitment to the community. And, of course, the Hen did itself a fabulous business selling beer, stout ales, cider, wines, and a significant amount of whisky. The fair ran during a single weekend with an overwhelming positive reaction of the local populace. The Old Speckled Hen tent, a very good business decision with the cost of the free tent food offset by profits from the dining room and bar, created tremendous goodwill. The laird sent down his polished carriage to treat wide-eyed youngsters to a ride around the village streets. And so, the legacy of The Old Speckled Hen continued to be burnished.

Due to the obvious appeal of Cairie and her joy in making good food, the days of the Hen being a pub focused on the lower classes were now in the past and all customers made to feel welcome, regardless of the size of their tab. Other than the variety and quality of the food, most of the changes at the Hen under Cairie were subtle: the place fairly sparkled, so very clean; the mirror behind the bar polished weekly, making it stand out; and a personal warmth and happiness exuded from those who worked there. Cairie had become something of a local celebrity, and diners felt special when she made one of her now infrequent forays into the dining room, touching arms and recognizing the regular patrons.

And yet Cairie still felt unfulfilled. She had maintained discreet communication with the head chef of her old restaurant in Paisley, who had a network of contacts within the finer trade in south and west Scotland. The young chef had been in Dalry some five years now, and in her late twenties she hoped for grander things. Through Andrew, the Paisley chef had secretly learned of a superb opportunity in the capital city of Edinburgh. And the two of them knew what to do.

Sometime later, on a Sunday evening as they were closing the kitchen of the Hen, Cairie approached William Collins and motioned for him to sit.

She removed her toque, shook out the locks of her ginger hair, smiled shyly, and said, "I want you to know I have decided to take my leave in two weeks. I shall be moving to Edinburgh, and you will need to get a new chef to manage your kitchen. You gave me a tremendous opportunity here and I am truly grateful. I have done what I had hoped for, and it is time for me to move on."

Colly was thunderstruck and for a time could only move his lips, unable to form any words. Cairie had made up her mind in a blindingly clear manner, having thought the idea through, so he sighed and nodded.

She said, "I have a wonderful chance to run a private dining room in the prestigious, old New Club on Princes Street in Edinburgh. The focus will be on elegant meals served five nights a week to the members and their guests, in addition to supervising a luncheon service and a team of four other chefs. It is an opportunity I cannot let pass."

Not in Colly's nature to feel anger at Cairie's decision, he stood and gave her a warm hug.

"Will you help me in making arrangements for another chef?" he asked plaintively.

"Of course I shall," she said. "Be aware I will not be able to stay more than two weeks, under any circumstances."

The next few days were a whirlwind of activity. Colly immediately informed his minority partners of the change, and neither Fiona nor the laird were surprised.

The laird said, "It is the nature of this business for people to do their part and then move on. Don't take it personally."

Colly took everything about the Hen personally. He still slept every night in the room on the second floor, although it had gradually been improved such that it had taken on the appearance of a hotel suite, with even the little office now first rate. The Hen staff relationships were business and not familial; nonetheless, Cairie's leaving bothered him. He was fully and personally invested in running the pub, while others saw the work as a means of supporting themselves economically.

After some fits and starts, Cairie had convinced Colly to consider her assistant Brian Stewart as a replacement. Brian, a solid, competent cook, possessed none of the artistic flair Cairie brought to the Hen. Colly, a realist, understood Cairie had been a rare find. In the transition he needed someone loyal he could trust, such as Brian.

They put together a fine send-off celebration for Cairie, with plentiful haggis, puddings, mincemeat tarts, bangers, sausage rolls, meat pies, scones, and shortbreads, set out in a grand buffet in the dining room at the Hen. Colly and Cairie held court with the loyal customers, and Brian was fine-looking in his classic chef's attire. The focus remained on food, not alcohol, even though there was much imbibing nonetheless.

The next morning, the laird sent his carriage to haul Cairie to the rail station. The train was to transfer her to Glasgow and then on to Edinburgh. Cairie had packed her knives and recipes in a valise; the remainder of her clothing and possessions were in a trunk in the back of the carriage. She wished Brian the best luck with the Hen, and then, embracing Colly and kissing his cheek—which caused him to blush vividly—she climbed into the carriage and sped off.

It is difficult to comprehend how unique these happenings were for a young Scottish professional woman in the mid-nineteenth century. The country faced turmoil from religious challenges, unemployment, the famine in Ireland which sent destitutes scrambling to Scotland for a chance in life, mechanization and modernization of weaving and mining, economic turmoil, continued dissension within government, and yet Cairie, seemingly oblivious, was eager to throw herself into life's latest opportunity.

Her train ride to Edinburgh, a city she had never visited, was interestingly calm. She had a level of confidence and optimism shockingly necessary for what she faced, an opportunity with rough edges. The New Club on Princes Street in Edinburgh was one of several elite private gentlemen's clubs in the capital city. It had a prime location, leather chairs, a stuffy atmosphere, and a dining room which had been run to ruin by the previous megalomaniac, who succumbed to the pressures of the members' unrealistic expectations. Cairie had a chance, but it was no sure thing.

The general manager of The New Club met Cairie at the train station and they shared a carriage ride to the building that housed the Club. Purpose built in the late 1830s, it replaced the former location in a building several blocks away, dating to the late 1700s, although it remained a nondescript structure of four stories. The ground floor had a high ceiling, and in the comfortable leather chairs the members lounged while reading books and newspapers by the light of oil lamps. They smoked cigars or pipes and sometimes enjoyed a drink or two in the late afternoon. Large fireplaces dominated both ends of the room, and in a bar area at the back, some members kept their private brands of spirits. It was quiet and restful, other than the occasional tinkle of glassware, with no raucous behavior tolerated. A cloakroom and the GM's office were located just inside the entrance.

On the second floor, reached by a broad staircase, the dining room held an uncrowded array of tables and chairs, and a piano off to one side. A hallway led to men's and ladies' water closets. The kitchen occupied the remainder of the floor. The third floor held several private dining rooms, the chef's quarters, and some administrative work areas.

The top floor consisted of a ballroom used for dances and members' meetings, and a kind of outdoor garden, utilized when the weather permitted gentlemen and ladies to stroll about for a bit of fresh air during pauses by the musicians.

Old Leonard, the general manager, directed an attendant to deliver Cairie's trunk to her quarters on the third floor, and then asked her to "Please follow me" as he climbed some back stairs to the kitchen.

On Monday afternoon, with the dining room closed that evening of the week, workers were cleaning up from the completed lunch service and stood as Old Leonard introduced the new head chef. Cairie calmly surveyed the crew, nodding and shaking hands when offered. She noted the usual assortment of assistant chefs, line cooks, a pastry chef, wine steward, two bartenders, porters, dishwashers, and several waiters. The previous head chef had succumbed to a tiff with some of the more demanding Club members in a bout of ego certain to be lost by the chef. The team could perhaps be salvaged. It remained to be seen how Cairie proceeded these first days, which set the tone for her prospects.

Realizing you get only one chance to make a first impression, Cairie spoke softly for several minutes about those things important to her: cleanliness, tidiness, attention to detail, respect for one another, making food which tasted good, while having fun doing it. For the next few hours she conducted brief yet intensely focused one-on-one meetings with the staff. She met with everyone, including the dishwashers, something noticed by all. She thanked everyone and bid them good evening, and then retreated to her quarters to recover from her trip and the stress of her new responsibilities.

Mornings at The New Club were quiet affairs with no breakfast service. At midmorning, tea and coffee were made available, along with toast and marmalade for any members who happened to be about. Lunch service started at noon, ending at half after two o'clock, typically including a special entrée of the day, with fresh soups and interesting salads like shallots and olives. Alcohol was available to the members and their guests, its use discreet during the day. Late in the afternoon, members arrived to relax and read the daily papers, play some cards, or have subdued conversations, while enjoying a whisky, gin, or glass of cider. Dinner service began at six thirty, lasting until nine thirty, only Wednesday through Sunday, giving the staff a couple of nights of relief. Dinners were well attended, with members and their guests filling the tables, especially on weekends, enjoying beer and wine with their meals. Some of the members were what could be called "fussy eaters," possessing what they deemed were discriminating palates. In truth, the most discerning diners didn't publicly crow about their gustatorial talents. However, The New Club was well known as a fine dining destination.

Cairie didn't rock the boat, so to speak, at first. She spent time getting to know the likes and dislikes of her members, as well as the talents and weaknesses of her staff. Old Leonard helped immensely with detailed private conversations, allowing Cairie to ask questions and develop her own sense of understanding of the membership. She was expected to be sensitive and discreet, with ego kept well in check. Her staff, especially the assistant chefs, were less helpful since she had not yet developed a sense of trust with them and they still remembered the sting of Andre having been fired for his contentious behavior in challenging the whims of certain members.

Both parties were in the wrong on that one—something to be remembered without focusing on it.

In a short time, Cairie's influence and leadership began to be noticed. The kitchen and serving areas were much cleaner, things sparkled, and everything had its proper place. Prep work was more orderly, which allowed for prompt service. Food temperatures were more optimal, and things began to taste better. The kitchen staff and waiters were now relaxed and polite. It seemed like a happier place. Cairie prevailed on Old Leonard to include her in the monthly meetings with the Operating Committee so she could develop a sense of expectations. A few members reacted negatively to the idea, yet in the spirit of supporting the new chef, acquiesced. The menu didn't need much work; the meal items were common for clubs of this rank, with attention to detail setting them apart. Cairie tried to come out with some new entrée or dessert every other month to create expectations.

After six months, Cairie convinced the committee to approve an increase in pay for her people. Members and staff alike noticed the gesture, recognizing the value of loyalty to the smooth operation of the Club.

Cairie matured in her professional life, the only life she had, after giving everything to the development of the craft of creating good food. She had no room for a personal life, such was her dedication to becoming a noted chef. She had taken only three days' leave when Ma Watts had passed away. Just enough time to transit to Cladich for the wake and burial. Her Ma was so proud of Cairie, but they had not had much time to share together since Cairie took the job in Dumbarton lo those many years ago. Ma made one visit to Cairie whilst she ran the kitchen at The Old Speckled Hen, and was simply shocked at the attention and adulation her only child received from the Hen's customers and co-workers. Ma took no credit for any influence she may have had on Cairie's upbringing.

"It is only my guid luck ah'm mak me happy!" she said in her thick North Country brogue, describing her joy at her daughter's successes.

Cairie's palate of skills slowly transformed the ordinary into the extraordinary, soon embraced enthusiastically by The New Club members. In the capital city of Scotland, it became the envy of those seeking status and pride. There had developed a level of trust between Cairie and the Operating Committee such that the relationship became more of a partnership than employment.

Fergus Ritchie, noted as the most discerning and cranky of the members, went out of his way to praise her: "Lass, you have made our Club a home away from home!"

Others chimed in, to the point of making Cairie embarrassed and forcing her to emphasize theirs was a professional relationship. The members were duly chastened by her comment and became keenly aware of how they subsequently treated and communicated with her.

Things with the staff went not quite as smoothly. In her quiet way Cairie began to change the way staff matters were resolved and established the "pecking order" as she saw it. While service time and loyalty were important, merit and creativity were more relevant in terms of organizational dynamics. An assistant chef left first, followed by a bartender of many years' standing, the departure of neither causing the slightest decline in order or quality. Shockingly, they were replaced by one of the line cooks and a waiter who, both yearning for self-improvement, threw themselves into the work. In culinary circles, The New Club kitchen became the most desirable place to work in southeast Scotland. This demand allowed Cairie to patiently improve overall staff quality without any real upheaval. While some members complained over the loss of their favorite staff persons, no one could argue against the fact that the service became immensely better.

After a year on the job, the Operating Committee rewarded Cairie with a hefty raise in pay and an unheard-of employment commitment requiring several months' notice requirement for replacement to be initiated. This gave Cairie real financial security for the first time in her life. She took a serviced apartment of her own in the famed Balmoral Hotel, a short walk down Princes Street from The New Club. Being able to put some distance between herself and The New Club kitchen brought a huge reduction in stress. In the evenings when The New Club dining room closed, she relaxed by walking the brightly lit Princes Street and gazing in the shops and restaurants ... a time for her to recharge, which also pointed out how alone she was in the vibrant city. She didn't need romance so much as she needed companionship from the opposite sex, other than staff or Club members, and such a situation was unlikely.

Then, unexpectedly, member Garrick McCaig, a prominent financier with Clydesdale Bank in Edinburgh, approached her. A polished individual, Garrick had a good education, and a limited ancestry—an often disqualifying requirement in those times in the Scottish banking business. Hard work, intellectual creativity, a suave manner, and good looks had allowed Garrick to reach the senior levels of the firm at a young age.

He had been tasked with hosting a dinner for the bank's board of directors and wanted Cairie to prepare a special evening meal for the group. It flattered Cairie, yet she kept her wits about her, seeking more details. Garrick had already sought and received dispensation from The New Club's Operating Committee to host the meal in the large private dining room off the ballroom on the Club's fourth floor. Old Leonard had committed to sprucing up the room with fresh candles, flowers, and clean drapes. Cairie had sole purview over the menu. Though excited over the project, she was dismayed to learn she had only a fortnight to prepare. She leapt to the challenge, with the proviso she would consult with Garrick daily until the dinner.

And so, each day after completing the Club's lunch service, she trudged over the two blocks, to the bank building on George Street, climbed two flights of stairs and spent a couple of hours with Garrick, reviewing her plans. The consummate professional, she reviewed a seating chart, making sure enemies weren't seated near each other, questioning likes and dislikes, meal and wine budgets, and a myriad of details which meant the difference between good and great. Garrick nodded, gave opinions, asked questions, and so forth, the entire time they met.

Garrick had an ulterior motive. Never married, he had been noticing Cairie the whole time she had worked at The New Club. A very attractive and comely woman, Cairie had a reputation as being professionally aloof with Club members, avoiding personal contact; she felt it to be unprofessional. So, a kind of left-handed courtship began between Garrick and Cairie.

The day of the dinner finally arrived, cold and overcast with a hint of snow, and Cairie beside herself with nervous excitement. She had prepared many fancy dinners in the past, with this the first one in which she acted as a true artist on display. Careful not to let any of the preparations detract from the meal service to the regular members' evening meal, her planning and prep work allowed most of the staff to have some hand in Garrick's special meal. The table had been covered with fresh linens, the chairs cleaned and polished, special candelabra were employed with trimmed beeswax candles, two large floral arrangements graced the table, the fine china embossed with The New Club coat of arms was ready, the silver neatly arranged in order of use, and the crystal wine and water goblets fairly sparkled. The board meeting ended at five, with the dinner planned for half after six.

The gentlemen began arriving and enjoyed cocktails at the first-floor bar, chatting and making idle talk. They had been to innumerable business dinners, but had no idea what they were in for. At the appointed time Garrick rounded them together and they made their way to the fourth floor, where Old Leonard greeted them and made sure they were comfortably seated. Two waiters were filling water goblets and asking each diner if they preferred a German white or a French claret as wine with the meal, replacing the crystal as required. Cairie lurked behind the scenes; the process of moving the various dishes from the second to the fourth floor while maintaining optimum temperatures required smooth coordination.

Garrick called for attention, said a few words of welcome, and the meal began. The first course, walnut oatcake crackers with a tangy cheddar spread, was served with honeyed figs so delicious several attendees licked their fingers. The plates were removed and replaced with bowls of Cullen Skink, a thick and velvety smoked fish soup perfect for a dinner on a cold evening. These proper gentlemen fought the urge to smack their lips in delight. The bowls were replaced with heaping plates of potatoes and turnips, to fill the need for a starch. Then the waiters wheeled out a cart with a steaming pair of fresh haggis, that delicate pudding from a sheep's pluck, a mixture of heart, liver, lungs, minced onion, oatmeal, suet, spices, and salt—lovingly encased in the animal's stomach in which it had baked for hours. The men tucked into the haggis as if they had not eaten in days; this course took a while since the enjoyment of a haggis is not to be rushed. This was followed by lamb sausage: succulent patties tender and flavorful, with the perfect amount of tangy lemon and sweet mint, topped with a delectable whisky cream sauce which the diners mopped up with crusts of fresh bread. After a slight pause, Cairie came in pushing a cart with the climax dessert: a creamy, layered, traditional trifle pudding laced with whisky, custard, jelly, and preserved tart raspberries.

Resplendent in her chef's attire, Cairie had donned a double-breasted white jacket with black buttons, hound's-tooth pants, and a toque blanche on her head. The men rose as a group and applauded the chef, who beckoned towards the hall. Her entire staff came into the room to share in the adulation. After the dessert was finished, tea and coffee were served, with some of the men retiring to the open rooftop porch for a glass of port and a cigar in the brisk night air.

The tables were being cleaned and Cairie chatted with some of the men, when Garrick approached her, gushing with praise and appreciation.

"However can I thank you?" he said to Cairie, who responded, eyes twinkling with a bit of a flirty smile: "I'm sure you will figure something out, Garrick."

The romance began.

The first date was ever so innocent; after the board dinner he invited her for an evening meal on one her nights off. Garrick was confused as to what to suggest—where do you dine with a famous chef? He thought perhaps the dining room at the Balmoral Hotel, but was uncomfortable with their first private time together being in the place where she made her lodging. He smartly asked where Cairie preferred to go, and she surprised him by suggesting they walk to a Chinese place a few blocks away, kind of a hole in the wall.

There, an Asian man seated them at a table for two and promptly returned with a white porcelain, red dragon design pot of green tea and two matching cups. She smiled at the man, who blushed in recognition and said he would serve them the usual.

So, this must be one of Cairie's haunts when on her own, Garrick thought, when she didn't want high-end service or food which needed to be scrutinized. She sought simple food and relaxation.

In no time they were served steaming bowls of noodles in broth, which they ate with chopsticks; Cairie taught Garrick their proper use. This was followed with boiled fish—heads and tails—served over rice, with vegetables. They ate and ate, chopsticks flashing, laughing and talking, avoiding the embarrassment normally associated with a first date, relaxed and being themselves, wonderful for them both. It is always fun to be who you are, not trying to play a role or meet someone else's expectations.

After the meal, the Chinese man, Nyan Fatt Lee, came to the table and wished them a good evening, and said the meal would be his gift to Cairie and her guest.

Garrick tried to protest. Cairie put her hand on his and said, "Just say thank you."

Afterwards, they walked about the quiet city in a light snow for a short while and then Garrick took Cairie back to the Balmoral, kissing her goodnight on the cheek before she left to walk up the steps to her apartment. He waited until she reached the top of the stairs, where she turned and smiled and, with a wave, disappeared. What a lovely start!

The courtship of Cairie Watts by Garrick McCaig would be an affair closely watched and supported by those who knew them. In their early thirties, they both had so far managed a singular focus on their careers, to the extent they neither had much of a normal social life. They were respected for their professional achievements, while they subconsciously hungered for social contact with the opposite sex. This resulted in a romance so intense they overwhelmed each other. Neither had siblings nor surviving parents, so they had no required approvals to overcome. They were nonetheless proper, lest their behavior tarnish their well-achieved reputations.

As the relationship approached six months, they knew one another well enough as to make honest, sincere commitments to each other. They were married one Saturday afternoon in the ballroom of The New Club, an event attended by Club members, Cairie's kitchen staff, and Garrick's partners and wives. William "Colly" Collins presented the bride, assisted by his wife, the former Willa Cather, both in for the event from Glasgow. The service was joyous, but not glamorous. In deference to Cairie's innate need to manage things culinary, it included no prepared food, only glasses of sparkling wine.

The young twosome decamped to Garrick's fashionable flat on Dundas Street, off Princes Street Gardens. They took a few days' journey into the central Highlands as a honeymoon.

As with newly married couples starting out, it took some time for Cairie and Garrick to sort out each other's schedules. Garrick McCaig functioned as a senior partner, at a young age, for a prominent bank, which meant late nights and some travel. Cairie Watts McCaig ran the culinary side of a renowned men's club, also now in demand to prepare food for outside special events including the occasional formal government affair. This meant they had to work hard to make their marriage seem normal, formally scheduling time for themselves.

And so the days and weeks and months passed, and the love between the two of them grew deeper. They were happy with things and hoped to continue in this manner for the foreseeable future. But this is not the way real life works.

Two years into the couple's fairytale relationship, Old Leonard asked for some private time with Cairie, a bit unusual although they had a good relationship that was professional more so than personal. Cairie, though puzzled, went to his office at the agreed time.

Old Leonard closed his office door. His face awash with anguish, tears filled his eyes. He said, "I am faced with a tragic situation and seek your counsel."

The man's shoulders slumped as the story rushed out of him. Paola, a middle-aged Italian woman, worked in the accounts department at the Club. Her husband, a Scottish stonemason named John Adams, had been tragically killed in a construction accident a few years prior and Paola had been faced with raising their daughter by herself. Paola, a good employee, an honest, hard worker, kept to herself and provided as best she could for her daughter, Jesse, now aged nine. A few days before, Paola had approached Leonard, seemingly stricken about a private matter. She had been having some pain and discovered a large lump in her breast. She immediately went to a physician, who advised her she had advanced breast cancer, with at most a few weeks to live. Her remaining time could be painful and she would not be able to work. She had come to Leonard in a desperate state of mind, fearful of how to manage and terrified at the prospect of Jesse being sent to an orphanage. Paola had no relatives or close friends to turn to. Leonard offered her reassurance: to relieve her mind, her pay would continue through to the end, and a home would be found for young Jesse. Leonard wanted Cairie to help him sort out what to do with the young girl, while keeping the matter private.

Cairie didn't blink, only saying, "Let me talk to Garrick."

Cairie went and put on her coat, taking leave of the Club for a short while. She walked through a light rain the few blocks to Clydesdale Bank, into the lobby, and climbed the stairs to Garrick's office. The staff were shocked to see Cairie, who almost never came to the bank. Well liked, they warmly welcomed her. Garrick's assistant, Alison, showed Cairie into his corner office and went to fetch Garrick from a meeting, anxious over the look on Cairie's face.

In a few minutes, Garrick, looking worried and concerned, came rushing into his office. "What is it, darling? It must be something dreadful for you to come here, midafternoon, in the rain!" he said as he sat next to her on the couch.

Expressionless, Cairie faced Garrick and said, "I want us to take in a young girl as our own."

To say Garrick had been dumbstruck underestimated his shock and surprise.

He loved Cairie like no one else in the world, so with typical Scottish flair he said, "Tell me more."

The story of the situation came flowing out of Cairie as a mixture of fear, sadness, and excitement. She had never enjoyed the luxury of time for a real family or ever considered having her own child; life had been a self-centered quest for a perfect culinary career. And in her mid-thirties she now had second thoughts about needing a more complete life. She could cut back a bit on her work outside The New Club, freeing the time to shelter and nurture someone other than herself and Garrick. They agreed to discuss the matter at length back in their flat later. Cairie went back to The New Club kitchen and carried on as normal for the remainder of the day.

That evening, Cairie brought home a tureen of soup from The New Club for their late supper, served with crackers and white tea. When they had eaten, Cairie cleared her throat and reaffirmed her desire to provide a home for Jesse Adams. Ever the practical Scotsman, Garrick patiently went through the reasons why this should not make sense, particularly their lack of experience in child-rearing and the potential appearance as some seemingly selfish, albeit admirable, act of vanity.

"The real question to be answered is: Are *we* committed to providing a life for this child?" said Garrick, with an emphasis on the implied "us."

Neither Garrick nor Cairie had ever been particularly religious—not that they were atheists, mind you. They decided they should have a chat with someone with more experience in matters of religion and ethics. Garrick reached out to Roddy Hamilton, who held a senior position in the Kirk, as the Church of Scotland was known in some circles.

Late the next afternoon, Garrick and Cairie were led into Hamilton's office, located in the Synod's administrative center. Roddy could not have been more helpful, reviewing the pros and cons of taking in a child.

"You are honest, sober people, whose only apparent vice is working too hard! Yours should be a wonderful, loving home."

In the final analysis, he said, "God gives us opportunities to live our faith, and we need to embrace them."

The next morning, Cairie reached out to Old Leonard, asking him to have Paola come to his office. After a proper introduction, Cairie advised them both of her and Garrick's desire to provide a loving home to Jesse Adams. Paola broke down, the relief shuddering through her pain-wracked body. Old Leonard simply nodded, his judgment in gauging the goodness and character of others having been affirmed. They decided that Paola should break the news to Jesse herself, since the young child knew nothing of her mother's medical condition and could be overwhelmed by the changes taking place.

Children are resilient, and all concerned were hopeful Jesse could develop a comfortable relationship with Cairie and Garrick before her mother passed. Cairie began to meet with the child daily and on the weekends they spent an afternoon together, Paola and Jesse, Garrick and Cairie. They made for an incongruous group: Paola and Jesse, olive-complexioned, with dark hair, and Cairie, rosy-cheeked, with ginger hair, and Garrick, tall and sandy-haired, with a deep Glasgow accent. The knowledge that they had to make the situation work helped overcome their fears and nervousness. Cairie had prepared a room in their flat on Dundas Street, where Jesse began to infrequently stay. They needed to find a school nearby, although there was no need to rush. Within a few weeks, the cancer took Paola and her pain ended. Jesse grieved, but she did so in the loving arms of Cairie and Garrick.

The couple made the adjustment to becoming parents. Their schedules became less fluid and they made time for the three of them to be a family. Cairie had the biggest change and it showed in the amount of time she committed to The New Club. Noticed, and not very favorably, by the Club's Operating Committee, who were irritated that they had not been consulted beforehand, and took Old Leonard to task.

His spine stiffened, and he rose from his meeting chair as he spoke: "Gentleman, Cairie Watts McCaig has an impeccable reputation in this city and this region. She can walk into the finest dining establishments in Scotland, or England, for that matter, and have her situation accommodated. I suggest you be thankful she is loyal to you!" Old Leonard then left the room.

After some muttering, finally, one individual said, "I suggest we adjourn,"—the last of the discussion on this matter.

They made quite a trio. Jesse Adams going through a tumultuous time for a young girl, with the loss of her mother, the upheaval in her life, and the hormonal changes preteens experience. Yet, she had a good head on her shoulders and knew it in her interest to make the situation work. Some evenings she took her schoolwork and sat in an alcove off The New Club kitchen, out of the way, making use of her time and watching how others treated her new mother. Cairie carried herself proudly in her work and smiled continuously, reflecting the attitude she had developed about life for some time. When the evening rush began to slow down, she took a hamper and created a meal for the three of them.

They arrived back at the flat about the time Garrick returned from his office and they broke bread together, everyone sharing the details of their day. For several months, things went well, and they slowly became a loving family. The biggest change being Garrick, who wore none of his officious office manner when with his two ladies. He removed his jacket and tie, and Cairie and Jesse saw an almost visible relaxation wash over his body. Not what one called a "homebody," nevertheless he accepted the role of husband and father with relish. Cairie had managed to maintain a level of commitment acceptable to The New Club Operating Committee and the membership in general. The new family had established a level of stability.

Then, one Friday, late in the afternoon, Garrick suddenly appeared in the kitchen of The New Club as Cairie busily minced onions for a reduction to accompany that evening's dinner special. Startled at seeing Garrick, she immediately thought he must be bringing bad news. And, in a sense, he was. He asked Cairie whether they could talk privately. In the midst of the rush of preparations for one of the Club's busiest dinner evenings, she wiped her hands on her apron and motioned him into an alcove, after nodding to her two under-chefs to keep the momentum going. Without a door on the alcove, the sounds of a kitchen in action filtered around them.

"Cairie, I couldn't wait to talk with you. The firm has asked me to move to London and open an investment house in the city. It is the opportunity of my lifetime, but means us picking up and relocating, and you leaving your dream job at The New Club. I think it may be a chance for us to have a normal life with Jesse," Garrick blurted out in nervousness, excitement, and fear.

Dumbfounded, Cairie had trouble finding her voice. She had never contemplated such a disruption in their lives. Garrick, in an expression of love, deferred to what Cairie decided as being best for them; he had always made sure the family came first. Cairie grabbed Garrick, wrapping her arms tightly around him as she kissed him on the mouth.

"We will talk when I get home," she said. "Please go take care of Jesse and don't mention a thing. Act as normal as possible."

She flew back into the kitchen, giving orders as if this was a normal night. Garrick and Jesse were asleep when she came into the flat late that evening. The night had been a blur of activity and emotions for Cairie. Once at home, she relaxed and lay next to Garrick before going into a deep and restorative sleep.

The next morning, they awoke for early tea and scones. Both Cairie and Jesse peered at Garrick as he read the paper. When he laid it aside, stern-faced with the hint of a smile, the two of them had learned to anticipate his tenderness.

As Jesse slowly licked the last of the clotted cream and strawberry jam from her fingers, Garrick softly said, "Jesse, Cairie and I have a family matter to discuss with you."

Cairie straightened her back and smoothed her robe, saying, "Jesse, Garrick has a work opportunity which requires me to leave The New Club, and for us to move to England, in the city of London. We want to know what you think of such a situation."

Jesse looked about and, with dark eyes shining, as preteens are wont to do, said, "You mean you being home with me, like the mothers of my friends?"

With that simple statement, Jesse set in motion a change in their lives.

Always knackered, Cairie had become worn down by the work at The New Club—the hours, the demands of the members, the constant quest for perfection, seeking the subtle tastes which caused diners to exclaim and swoon and smile. In the beginning, it consumed her whole life; now she had a husband who loved her and a child who needed her, and that which she had been subconsciously wrestling with had in fact become a reality. She viewed it as a fortuitous opportunity, the kind of thing which changes lives forever, and they were going to embrace it.

She took Old Leonard into her confidence, describing the tumultuous change ahead. They developed a plan for dealing with the Operating Committee later in the week, since they had no time to waste. The Clydesdale Bank wanted to announce the planned opening of the London office to the trade. Old Leonard added to the formal agenda, an item of "new business" discreetly placed near the end of the meeting. When other business had been addressed and with the time at hand, Old Leonard recognized Cairie, who stood and calmly addressed the group.

"Many of you know Garrick and I recently undertook the formal adoption of the child of a former Club staff member. Whilst it has been my hope to continue as your executive chef, matters have arisen which cause me to announce my leave, which will be taken within the next couple of months. I thank the Club for giving me my chance, and will endeavor to assist Leonard in finding and engaging my suitable replacement."

Cairie excused herself and left the stunned men to their discussion.

The transition went quite smoothly. Garrick went to London and leased them a handsome flat in Mayfair, a short carriage ride from the Financial Center where the Clydesdale Bank had secured a modest suite of offices. Garrick threw himself into the process of establishing the base of the business, making contacts and appointments, returning to Edinburgh each fortnight, thoroughly exhausted.

Cairie tended to Jesse's needs and kept the kitchen and dining service afloat at The New Club. As expected, tremendous interest arose from those who sought to take over the fine business Cairie had established. Several of them were charlatans—only eager to exploit an opportunity—which Cairie and Old Leonard sniffed out and disposed of. They finally narrowed it to three male candidates, and Cairie excused herself from the process, feeling further participation improper. Within a week they selected a young chef from Glasgow who could start immediately. Cairie assisted Old Leonard and the new chef in the transition over a week's time, and then it was done.

She walked home the few blocks to their flat on Dundas Street, where Jesse met her with a big hug. She placed her double-breasted white jacket, hound's-tooth pants, and toque in a closet, her knife kit in its special box, let out a deep sigh, and began her new life as a wife and mother.

The family had decided to keep the Edinburgh flat, leasing it out against the expectation they may possibly return at some future date during Garrick's career. The bank provided London accommodations for them, so it wasn't much of a risk. Jesse had school each day while Cairie busied herself with packing those belongings going to London instead of storage. Neither she nor Garrick had focused on material things, and Jesse had never been in a position to afford them. Still, there were those gewgaws or reminder tokens, if you will, of their lives: a hairpin Ma Watts had gifted Cairie when she left Cladich; a medal Garrick had won as a student in an oratorical contest; and a rattle Paola had purchased for baby Jesse—things worth little monetarily, yet priceless. Enjoying free time she had never had, Cairie lovingly wrapped these and other things, placing them in a special box. They were taking no furniture, mostly clothing and a precious few rotogravure pictures, and, of course, Cairie's cherished chef's knives.

Garrick found the time at home with his two ladies always precious indeed. Arriving on the evening train every other Friday, after a six-hour trip from London's King's Cross, he walked the short distance from the Waverly train station to Dundas Street, where Cairie and Jesse anxiously awaited. After hugs and kisses, they went the short distance from the flat, to dinner at Nyan Fatt Lee's Chinese place, which held a special significance for Cairie and Garrick. He, excitedly effusive, told them of the happenings in London over the past fortnight. They spent a slow weekend relaxing and being a family again, taking walks in the park and sometimes attending a Sunday service at the Kirk. On Monday morning, early, the trip reversed, with Garrick in his office by midafternoon. It went on like this for several weeks, except for the rare occasions when Garrick worked from the bank's Edinburgh offices on George Street—weeks everyone enjoyed.

Finally came the time for them to move to London. Cairie went to the bank and gave the keys to the flat to Alison, who oversaw the letting and management of the property. At The New Club she had an emotional goodbye with Leonard, hard for her; the gentleman had been her staunch advocate. Cairie gathered Jesse from her school, where the young girl gave a wave of departure to her teacher and classmates.

Then Cairie and Jesse, filled with excitement and apprehension, became two girls on the train. Neither had visited London, at the time a great civilized city teeming with people, cultures, carriages, smoke, sounds and smells, and the seat of government of one of the most powerful monarchies ever to exist. A great relief overcame them, to spot Garrick waiting on the platform when their train arrived.

In these times, there were deep-seated suspicions and jealousies between Scots and the English, going back generations. Cairie and Garrick decided to ignore them in order to maintain open minds in the interest of objectivity for Jesse, she at a particularly impressionable age. They were going to assimilate, as a family, into the spirit of London. Garrick had arranged for Jesse to attend a proper girls' school, to which she wore a tidy uniform each day. With no career to manage now, Cairie functioned as just another "mum" interested in seeing her child get the best chance in life. Make no mistake. Their financial situation provided Jesse with exposure to others also with one leg up on the world. They did not wear their good fortune on their sleeves, yet did associate with those who, through hard work and good luck, enjoyed a better life. No household in Mayfair made many sacrifices. Garrick's work had certain social responsibilities which couldn't be avoided, and opportunities involved the family, although Cairie oversaw what types of exposure Jesse received. Cairie was repulsed by elitist behaviors, having observed so many during her stint at The New Club. Garrick agreed; he felt proper values were more important than social position. So the family danced around some invites they felt reeked of ostentation. For the most part, though, they enjoyed a prosperous life in the city.

Their fashionable neighborhood of clean buildings—save for coal soot—and numerous leafy trees and shrubs, lent itself to walks, window shopping, and rare glimpses of the royal family. They were supportive of Queen Victoria, due to her strict standards about personal morality. Victoria had become reclusive since the death of her mother, another Victoria, and her husband Prince Albert, so royal sightings normally involved her children. These were happy times for the family from Edinburgh. Then real life intruded one more time.

Garrick had become phenomenally successful in London within a short time, but with the achievements came stresses to continue to perform. There had been casual conversation that the London posting constituted a trial to see whether Garrick had the guile and intelligence to become the next managing director of Clydesdale Bank. He felt the pressure, which only abated when with his girls, where he focused seemingly on being the best husband and father he could be.

On a rainy Thursday, around noon, Cairie heard a knock on the door of their flat. Fearing something had happened to Jesse, she flung open the door to find Colin Montgomery, Garrick's most trusted aide, standing in the doorway with a flushed face and holding his hat as his overcoat dripped onto the hall carpet.

"Mrs. McCaig, you need to come with me quickly. Your husband has suffered an attack!" said the flustered gentleman.

Cairie grabbed her coat and an umbrella and ran down the steps to the landing, where a horse carriage awaited. They literally flew down the crowded streets, arriving in front of the National Neurological Hospital, a facility which specialized in treating stroke victims.

They rushed to the second floor and went to a room crowded with doctors in white coats and nurses—nuns, actually—wearing white, heavily starched cornettes over dark tunics. Garrick lay unconscious on a bed, covered by a sheet. One eye protruded with the side of his face limp, also an arm and a leg seemed useless. A bit of drool flowed from his mouth, and a physician listened through a stethoscope placed on Garrick's chest and neck. Everyone in the room acted nervous and worried. Cairie didn't say a word, simply pulling a chair next to the bed, lifting the hem of her dress to wipe away the drool, and then grasping Garrick's hand in hers. The physician softly explained to Cairie how Garrick had suffered a massive stroke and what they were able to do at this point was give him comfort. Colin stayed in the background for a bit and then left, explaining he needed to arrange to have someone meet and care for Jesse as she returned from school. Stoic, Cairie sat with Garrick until late in the afternoon, when his spirit slipped away. He never regained consciousness, nor made any indication he knew of his situation or Cairie's presence.

Nearly overwhelmed, Cairie Watts McCaig exhibited no hysteria or loss of control. Her focus now had to be on Jesse. She left the body of her beloved husband in the care of the hospital, knowing the bank could handle the messy funeral details. Cairie took the carriage back to Mayfair. Climbing the stairs to their flat, Cairie could hear Jesse's sobbing through the door. When she walked in, she saw an ashen-faced Colin as Jesse rushed to her mother, grasping Cairie around the waist, her body wracked with sorrow.

"I didn't mean to tell her, Mrs. McCaig, I swear," said the stricken Colin.

Cairie waved him away with an "It's okay, please let us be now" expression.

She collapsed into a chair, rocking Jesse on her lap, offering reassurance and comfort to the young girl who had lost her third parent in a short amount of time. And Cairie had lost her husband, the love of her life, after a too brief marriage. They held on to one another until dark, when Cairie made them a bit of broth to share. That night Jesse slept in the big bed with Cairie, both hoping this a bad dream they would soon awaken from.

The next morning Cairie naturally kept Jesse home from school, wanting her close by to be able to provide each other with comfort, as need be. Midmorning, Colin arrived with the office manager, to help Cairie plan how to proceed. They presumed she wanted Garrick's body to be returned to Edinburgh for a proper funeral. Cairie was barely familiar with London, having resided there with Garrick and Jesse a scant eight months, and still adjusting to the role of serving as Jesse's mother. The firm would handle the funeral arrangements and relocate the two of them back to Edinburgh. When things were settled a bit, Cairie could decide on a path forward.

The following morning Cairie packed two bags, one for each of them, and they departed the London flat. They had the carriage stop at Jesse's school, where she went in to bid her friends and teachers goodbye. A tearful scene ensued, albeit necessary in order to begin to gain closure on the disastrous end of their London adventure.

The train ride to Edinburgh felt like it took forever, although in reality it was only six hours. With their flat on Dundas Street having been let on a term lease when they relocated to London, the bank housed them in the Balmoral Hotel in Cairie's old set of rooms. Roddy Hamilton himself performed the funeral for Garrick in a few days, at the Kirk. A number of Garrick's colleagues stood and sang his praises, and warm comments came from local friends the two of them had made together. Cairie insisted Old Leonard sit in the family pew along with her and Jesse, in addition to Colly and Willa Cather Collins, who had made the trip down from Glasgow. It was a somber event for them all and tears were shed. Colly and Willa insisted the two promise to visit them in Glasgow within the next few weeks.

The bank treated the two of them very fairly. Garrick's partnership assets were placed into an account for Cairie, and the bank established a special minor account for Jesse, with her mother as the trustee, with a contribution from the bank in the amount of five thousand pounds sterling. Combined with the income from the rental of the flat on Dundas Street, Garrick's girls were not financially vulnerable for the foreseeable future. Edinburgh, a different place without Garrick, every day somehow reminded Cairie and Jesse of the loss they had suffered. Although the firm subtlety pressured them to stay in Edinburgh out of an earnest regard to be sure they were taken care of, Cairie felt smothered by the attention. She needed to place Jesse back in school and wanted it to be where they had some assurance of staying for a while, to once again establish stability. Cairie felt the need for a brief trip to Glasgow to visit the Collins family.

William "Colly" Collins had moved to Glasgow when his Old Speckled Hen pub enterprise in Dalry had been sold. He served on the advisory board of Robert Livingston's consortium of companies, at the generous invitation of the man who had backed Harry Bailey's purchase of the Hen. The sale had left Colly well off, and he spent most of his time in a fevered courtship of Willa Cather, a legal assistant at Gerald Dickson's law firm in the Glasgow city center. Willa, an attractive, never married, middle-aged woman, worked in the law office to support herself and her elderly father. Captivated by Colly for his pleasant manner, honest approach, and dapper dress, she stood a head taller than him, which made the pair seem a bit incongruent. Colly had fallen hard, and, ever the gentleman, he stayed by Willa's side through the end of her father's illness. Only then did he propose marriage, which Willa gratefully accepted. They moved to a suite of rooms at a fashionable address on Queen Street and enjoyed life.

When Cairie and Jesse arrived in Glasgow for their visit, Colly and Willa overwhelmed them with graciousness. The only conditions set were that they were to pay for everything. Cairie and Jesse protested, but not much. They knew these offers were an expression of love best accepted.

"You two are like my daughter and granddaughter," Colly boasted.

Willa beamed at her husband's pride. She did her best to squire the girls around Glasgow, shopping and seeing the sights, a different luncheon spot each day. Evenings meant a fine dinner at some fashionable place, although one night Cairie made a luxurious haggis to remind them of the old times and their fine Scottish heritage.

One day Willa took Jesse to an art gallery, only the two of them, which gave Colly and Cairie some time alone. They went to Colly's men's club for the lunch sitting, in the area where women were allowed. A couple of gentlemen came over to the table to offer condolences. Having previously dined in The New Club, they held Cairie in some reverence. Colly, justly proud of her as if she were his daughter, exhibited a huge smile after the men left.

"Willa and I are prepared to set you up in a fine dining establishment here in Glasgow. With your food and my connections, success is assured," said Colly.

Tears formed in Cairie's eyes as she thanked Colly; she had other ideas. Out of a protective nature or maybe even out of fear, Cairie had decided to return to the security of the North Country which she had left some two decades previously. There she felt she could instill in Jesse the love and comfort of place she had enjoyed as a young girl.

They arranged to have their things packed in Edinburgh and shipped via train to Glasgow, where Colly watched to see they were collected and forwarded by horse drayage. Mostly clothing, some books and personal items, photogravures and remembrances of Garrick and Paola, recipe books, and her precious knife kit, they were a connection to life as Carrie and Jesse had known it. Interestingly, it included almost nothing which recalled their lives in London, as if it were a time they wanted to leave behind despite the fact that there, they were able to function as a normal family, at least for a while. Cairie and Jesse each carried a pair of valises with undergarments, toiletry items, and a few sets of clothes. Cairie had the wallet Garrick insisted she always carry, with identification, addresses, and currency against any unforeseen needs. They made quite a pair and did their best not to attract too much attention. The trip to Cladich from Glasgow took the better part of two days, along the beautiful, unusually sunny, coastal Scottish Highlands.

They traveled a long first day around to the north side of the Firth of Clyde, along Loch Lomond, and then down to Inveraray, where they spent the night sharing a bed in a roadside inn, after supping on a bowl of soup and a crust. They were not used to long, tiring carriage travel. Cairie made sure she chatted with Jesse often, aware of the disruption the child experienced.

"I want you to keep an open mind about this relocation," said Cairie. "We are going to need to depend on one another without reservation if we are to have any hope of happiness."

Jesse smiled and gave Cairie a hug. Cairie noticed Jesse becoming more expressive in her emotion towards her, with many displays of affection. They held one another throughout the night and enjoyed a restful sleep. The next morning after some oatcakes and tea, they made the last leg of the trip, to the north of Strathclyde and into the tiny village of Cladich, on the seaside of Oban in the coastal west Highlands.

There had been changes in the twenty-some years since Cairie left this place, which she had only visited in the interim when she came north to bury Ma Watts. In her grief, Cairie hadn't focused much on its environs or those who made it a village. After her time in large cities, she was struck by how much people interacted. Cairie and Jesse were trying to make the humble thatched cottage nice, where Cairie had been raised, which meant she had to reach out to neighbors who were at once friendly and at the same time skeptical of the city dwellers. However, everyone erred on the side of getting along. The local townspeople were proud of what Cairie had accomplished professionally—something of a celebrity, or at least a person who demonstrated you could rise and live your dreams if you tried hard enough and long enough.

Communication became one of the biggest things Cairie and Jesse coped with initially. With the dialect and pronunciation of the locals often so thick as to be nearly unintelligible, particularly so when uttered rapidly, in anger, or using slang:

"Ye gaun tae the gemme the night?"

"Naw."

"Naw? How no'?"

"Nae spondoolies."

"How did he get tae skip the queue, but no' us? Jammy bastard!"

In no time, they adjusted and fit in like locals.

Cairie planned to engage local craftspeople and see whether the thatched cottage, willed to her by Ma Watts and mostly sitting idle for these many years, could be made habitable to their standards. They were making do; clearly the condition of the structure meant a move to temporary lodgings in the interim. Cairie had in mind to update the whole cottage and add a special room for Jesse to call her own. Nearing her teens, she needed the privacy and security of her own space, a luxury in those times. After some polite inquiries at the church, Cairie engaged a carpenter to examine the cottage. The thatch needed to be freshened, of course, and relining of the fireplace chimney, plus the shoring up of a corner where the foundation had settled a bit. The structure was remarkably sound for one nearly two centuries or so in age. In order to add a room, Cairie had to approach a neighbor who hemmed and hawed about selling a tiny strip of property which practically meant nothing to the man.

"This smidgeon bit of land, ya know, may be critical to me at some time in the future, lest you think me a tool and kin find a way to mak me daftie!" said Fergus McGee to no one in particular, doing his best to demonstrate Scottish frugality in matters commercial.

Cairie finally sealed the deal by offering, in addition to a proper amount of cash, to boil him a fine haggis at a later date, for which she was still locally famous. The man's smiling red face became so broad with joy as to make Cairie blush.

And, in time, construction to modify the cottage began, with Cairie and Jesse taking lodging above the Cladich Inn for the interim. It was spartan lodging: a large room with two beds, a basin, and a chamber pot behind a screen in a corner. With no kitchen, they took meals with others in the inn's limited dining area. In short order, Cairie did a large portion of the cooking for the innkeeper, in return for their room and board. By the time work completed on the cottage, Cairie had built a significant trade at the inn, enough so that the owner begged her to continue. Cairie demurred, her priority to be there for Jesse, until the girl reached adulthood. As an accommodation, she agreed to continue to prepare the Saturday evening and Sunday noon meals with the proviso that Jesse help as a kind of hostess and waitstaff. Cairie reached out through some contacts and found a person to provide the weekday cooking chores so as not to leave the innkeeper in the lurch.

When they moved back into the reconditioned cottage, both Cairie and Jesse were thrilled with the privacy and warmth for the two of them, still sorting out a personal relationship free from stress and outside intervention. The main room with the fireplace now had a stone floor and the bedrooms wooden planks, with gleaming whitewashed walls throughout. The place smelled fresh and looked solid. Renderings of Garrick and Paola hung above the table where they dined, and mother and daughter never failed to offer remembrance as they gave thanks before each meal. A new stove, fueled with fragrant peat, sat in the kitchen alongside a sink and cistern pump, all quite cozy and comfortable.

The day started with them each handling personal hygiene issues, making their beds, and sharing bowls of porridge and a pot of tea. Then they bundled against the cold or the rain, depending as to what they saw outside the kitchen window. Cairie walked Jesse down the road to the schoolhouse, the same one Cairie had attended in her youth, and gave her a lunch packet.

Most of the day was spent on mundane living chores: laundry, cleaning, sewing, and shopping. In late afternoon she returned to the school and walked Jesse home, chatting about the day each of them had spent. They prepared the evening meal together and, in this manner, Cairie passed along to Jesse her artistry in the kitchen. Their dinners were often bold affairs with spices and sauces and many courses. Dining, a delight Cairie had forgotten about after spending so much time managing high-end kitchens, became the new treat. She provided Jesse a fine culinary education along the way and spent quality time with her daughter each day. After the rigorous task of cleaning the kitchen, Jesse finished her studies by oil lamp while Cairie sat beside her, enjoying the simplicity of the closeness. They may have been among the wealthiest of the local citizenry, while it wasn't worn on their sleeves.

One day, Jesse came home from school and asked if her mum could meet with the teacher. Alarmed, Cairie planned to visit midday the next and had Jesse carry the message.

"Do you have any idea what this is about?" Cairie asked Jesse, who in a classic, early teen response, merely shrugged her shoulders.

The next day, Cairie arrived at the school as the students were unwrapping their packet lunches from home. Miss Montgomery, the middle-aged teacher for the school, greeted her.

"I wonder if I might ask for your help?" the teacher said. "We are in something of a financial pinch due to an increase in students without a commensurate increase in funds. Perhaps we could arrange some type of fundraiser, with you heading the effort."

Cairie bit her lip for a moment, smiled, and said, "Please let me think this over for a day or so. I may have an idea."

She had been mulling for some time an idea for how she could help stimulate the citizenry to work to invigorate the village. She decided they should have a school fair and involve the whole community, not only those with children. Something over a weekend, with food, games, dancing, feats of strength, bake sale, raffle, and auction, all monies going into a special fund for the school. Kind of like the fall fair she had experienced in Dalry. This, of course, had to be done with the forbearance of the village council, who had a reputation of being resistant to change or anything new and not their idea. Still, Cairie felt confident she could win over the council.

At the school she shared the idea with Miss Montgomery, who thought it splendid. Cairie had written out a plan of action, which the teacher reviewed and offered some suggestions for improvement. Cairie appreciated the seriousness of the teacher and felt having a strong buy-in from the individual most affected by the funding shortfall would be important in presenting a persuasive case to the village council. The group met every fortnight in an evening session at the village hall, to discuss matters of importance or those required by the Crown for governing bodies. Stuart Mathieson, head of the Cladich Village Council, had been selected by the other councilors as the leader. Stuart, a stern, penurious older gentleman, was widely known for being particularly averse to any type of change or risk when it came to village funds. Cairie had her work cut out for her.

She managed to determine the rules by which the village council operated, including the need to have items placed on the agenda prior to any meeting. And she also knew that as a local taxpayer she had standing to raise issues, even though females were seldom recognized as being able to make serious contributions to the council's thinking.

At the evening meeting, Cairie arrived promptly, taking along Miss Montgomery to lend credibility. Old Stuart slowly went through the agenda in something of an unctuous manner, confidently in control of the outcomes.

"So, I see here, we have a matter to be brought before the council about the school, by a Mrs. McCaig," he said sourly. "Who might you be?"

Politely and with all the confidence she could muster, Cairie softly replied, "Councilor, my name is Cairstine Watts McCaig. I grew up in this village and attended the school, afterwards going away to pursue my lifework as a chef. By most accounts, I made accomplishments, culminating in the successful operation of the dining at the prestigious New Club in Edinburgh."

This caused some murmuring amongst the members of the council.

"After a time," Cairie said, "I married a partner in Clydesdale Bank and we relocated to London, taking with us our adopted daughter, Jesse. My husband Garrick then suffered an untimely death. In my grief, I have relocated with Jesse to the cottage I had here in Cladich, hoping I can impart to my child the joys and value of place I enjoyed here as a youth. My daughter attends the same school I attended, now carefully run by Miss Montgomery."

Cairie politely nodded at the teacher next to her, who returned the nod.

Cairie continued. "It has come to my attention that the number of students at the school has grown significantly over the last few years, while the funds available have remained stagnant, causing supplies and books to be insufficient."

At the mention of funds, Stuart and the others furrowed their brows and leaned forward in their chairs.

Cairie said, "I am here to ask for your approval of a fall fair to raise funds for the school. This will provide some supplemental support, without risk to the village of Cladich or this council."

This comment caused the councilors, save old Stuart, to visibly relax.

"Our thinking is a two-day event over a weekend, featuring food, games, dancing, feats of strength, bake sale, raffle, and auction, with the monies going into a special fund for the school, with no alcohol served, thereby minimizing any risk of rowdy behavior. It is a chance, besides the fundraising, to generate enthusiasm and bear witness to the value a village like ours brings to those who live here. We are hoping you will allow a date in October, when temperatures are moderate and before the rains come." Cairie sat down and nodded to the council.

With Cairie having finished proposing what appeared to be a wonderful idea, Grover McNeill raised his hand and proposed a motion of approval for the effort. The others nodded vigorously, except for Stuart, who felt the meeting being wrested from his control. He didn't see any way to argue against the matter without looking like more of a jackass than he already had a reputation for being. So, with a formal vote taken, Cairie and Miss Montgomery walked away, having achieved what many had thought impossible. And Cairie had established herself as a voice of reason to be reckoned with in Cladich.

A whirlwind of activity ensued with Cairie the obvious choice to be in charge since it would look unseemly for Miss Montgomery to have a role, due to potential conflicts. The local Church of Scotland allowed their site to be the central location for the festivities, including the use of their kitchen. Cairie was overwhelmed when word got out, at the level of participation the fair received from parents of students and other locals, proud for the chance to show their happiness in honor of both the school and the village of Cladich. Old Stuart wanted to claim control over any monies raised, but was shouted down by villagers who wanted the funds seen as an expression of love for the school and, by association, an investment in the future of Cladich. Cairie saw the management of the fair in the same manner she saw the management of any restaurant. Things were planned, tasks determined and assigned, and everyone took their responsibilities seriously.

The days of the fair finally arrived, with spectacular weather— sunshine and warmth, as well as could be hoped for. The whole town turned out, plus some townspeople from other villages in the area. A highlight of the year for the community, the fair proved a celebration for farmers, weavers, servants, domestics, and so forth—here also, a relief from their monotony and otherwise humdrum lives. They reveled in the sound of music, pipes and drums, some traditional Scottish games of strength, many contests, much dancing, and overall conviviality.

Cairie donned her chef's attire and turned out delectable dishes from the church basement kitchen. Wives and mothers baked their favorites, which were either sold or auctioned off, along with crafts, herbs, spices, and other household specialties. Jesse played a role, assisting in the collection of monies and parading around, displaying auction items held overhead while excitedly extolling their virtues or deliciousness.

The only negative was a townsman found operating a kind of shebeen from the back of a wagon in an alley in the village, selling homemade poteen, a kind of distilled spirit, in tiny jugs for those who felt alcohol a requirement for a good time. To his credit, Stuart shamed the scoundrel into giving the monies to the fund in return for avoiding being arrested for maintaining an unlicensed grogshop.

To everyone's shock and pleasant surprise, the Cladich Fall Fair raised an amount equivalent to half the annual budget for the school. The village council appointed a volunteer board to dispense the funds, which were placed in an account at the local bank. The board could spend the money as they saw fit for the school's needs and with the understanding that periodic reports would be posted for the public to see. This transparency assured the vibrancy of future fairs and the well-being of the school. Cairie, appointed as the first chairperson of the volunteer board, took pride in the responsibility. She had done Ma Watts proud. Colly and Willa had gotten wind of the fair and sent a contribution to the fund through the bank, in special honor of Cairie and Jesse.

Cairie and Jesse were now both established in the village. Jesse did well in her studies, which delighted her mother. Cairie, privately lonely, missed Garrick, who had been the person to offer her encouragement as well as tender love. Cairie and Jesse spent the Christmas holidays in Glasgow with Colly and Willa, nearly ten days of fun and frivolity. The two were villagers, no longer city dwellers, and were happy when they returned to life in Cladich, despite exhortations from the Collinses to stay on for a bit.

"We appreciate your kindness, but our lives are tied to the village now," said Cairie to Willa and Colly. "We hope you can understand."

Colly nodded solemnly to the girls, trying not to let his disappointment show.

Cairie became a bit bored in Cladich and needed more of a challenge than being a mum and a board chairperson demanded. She began to look for something to spend more time on. You can imagine that in a village of less than four hundred souls, opportunities were limited. Then she heard a rumor about a new hospital being planned on the Loch Awe, near the ruins of Kilchurn Castle. Kilchurn Castle had been the seat of the Campbells of Glenorchy, the most powerful branch of the Clan Campbell. Built in the mid-fifteenth century, it had stood in ruin since the late eighteenth century. The warlike scion, Sir Duncan Campbell, known as "Black Duncan," had represented Argyll in the Scottish Parliament, bringing fame and legitimacy to the area. The ruins, southwest of Dalmally, were a positive remembrance and often used as a directional point of reference. The rumor had the hospital being called Campbell House, with construction underway for the facility designed to provide regional health services, a scant three miles down the loch from Cladich.

Cairie decided to reach out to Colly to see if he could find out anything about potential opportunities for her—much like throwing a bone to a hungry dog, where Colly was concerned.

In response to her letter, Colly said, "My dear, if you need to work, why, Willa and I will establish you your own place, you know that."

"I'm not a person who wants a relaxing life. I feel I can make a contribution to the area without running a restaurant again," said Cairie. "I want you to reach out to some of your important contacts to see if there may be something I can provide to Campbell House, yet allow me to stay here in Cladich where I have made a life for Jesse and myself."

"I'll be back to you within a fortnight," said Colly.

Cairie felt it necessary to broach the subject of working again to Jesse, who had become quite a precocious young lady.

"Mum, I only have a couple of conditions," said Jesse. "No night work, and we stay in Cladich. Otherwise you will have my complete support."

Maintaining her social life and circle of friends had given Jesse a stability she had never before enjoyed in her young life. She had her birth mother's looks and her adopted mother's poise. Now taller than Cairie, she had long, dark hair and an olive complexion. In those times across the kingdom, dental hygiene had not been a priority for most citizens, who became known for tight-lipped smiles to hide their ugly, stained, and decaying bicuspids. Except for Jesse; she enjoyed good genes and brilliant, perfectly formed teeth. Suffice it to say she stood out in the coastal Scottish Highlands, attracting the attention of the more handsome of the boys. Cairie did not yet allow her to be courted, while young people have their ways of getting together to spend time. Cairie committed to not disrupting Jesse's life for quite a while.

As promised, Colly was prompt in his response to Cairie regarding opportunities surrounding Campbell House.

"My contact in Strathclyde regional government advises me they have been besieged by requests for preference regarding opportunities associated with Campbell House. I am able to drop in a few names and mentioned some favors owed, so in no time I arranged an audience for you with an official in Lochgilphead, who seems to be in charge of senior staffing," Colly said in a single breath. "He will be having meetings in Dalmally next week and wishes for you to join him for lunch on Tuesday. I trust you are available."

Shocked and overwhelmed at how quickly Colly had been able to cut through the bureaucracy, she immediately replied. "Of course, I will be available," said Cairie, and thanked Colly profusely.

Cairie arranged a carriage for the day-trip to Dalmally, excited to be back in the midst of professional activity. By now a beautiful, middle-aged Scottish woman with ginger hair and a natural complexion, Cairie dressed in a manner to enhance her appearance, which was focused on personal confidence rather than her radiance.

She left early on the Tuesday morning, disappointed to see wind and rain, but this was the coastal Highlands. Wearing a warm coat and clutching her sturdy umbrella, she waved goodbye to Jesse, who shouted good wishes as Cairie set off into the maelstrom. The surprisingly dry coach made pleasant the hour's ride as the weather morphed into a kind of soft mist on a gentle breeze.

Cairie arrived with time to spare and, after hanging her damp coat, entered into a conference room. Two men, one with a tight, high-collared suit, and a clerk of some sort came into the room. The men began to ask Cairie about her qualifications and experience. She told them of her career journey, culminating in the significant responsibility of running the dining facilities at The New Club. The clerk, feverishly taking notes, asked for Cairie to restate a couple things. It seems both men had dined at the Old Speckled Hen in Dalry, in times past, and remembered the sparkle and orderliness of the restaurant. The one gentleman, Seamus McGuirk, had friends from Edinburgh and had been made aware of the stellar reputation of The New Club under Cairie's watch. After a bit, he nodded to the other two, who promptly left the room. Service people came in and set up a table with a cloth, china, teapot, utensils, and a large tray of sandwiches, plus a tureen of soup.

"I hope you don't mind, Mrs. McCaig. My time in Dalmally is short, so I asked for lunch to be here, where we can talk privately," said Seamus.

He spoke in such a soft, pleasant, and kind manner, Cairie relaxed at this unusual behavior from a government official—many of whom had reputations as being officious, blunt, and self-important. The two enjoyed a pleasant lunch of the sandwiches and soup, albeit brief. Finishing their cups of tea with milk and sugar, Seamus got right to the point.

"Mrs. McCaig," said Seamus, to which Cairie promptly replied, "Please call me Cairie."

"Well then, Cairie. What I have in mind to discuss with you is a developing role planned for Campbell House. It is not yet fleshed out, and you must agree to help develop the proper description of the job. Campbell House is planned to be the finest regional hospital in the Scottish realm and will be used as the model for future facilities of its type. Historically, hospitals have not been known for either the variety or quality of the foods offered to patients. Nutrition is thought to be an area of potential significant improvement in patient satisfaction. We want someone to design a menu and oversee the preparation of the food by others, such as to impress patients and their families. Foremost, it is to hasten the improvement in their health, through to discharge. We are not sure at this time whether this is full-time work and are prepared to ensure a minimum of three days per week. Is this something you may be interested in?"

Briefly dumbstruck, Cairie perceived it as a role that used her talents and experience and yet still allowed her to lead a life outside of work. She clearly felt Colly had used his influence to define the perfect role for her. And the trip from Cladich would be shorter to Campbell House than Dalmally, making a commute possible. She tried to retain her composure and not burst forth with an acceptance.

"This seems like a very good opportunity for me. If I might have a day to discuss this with my daughter, might that be acceptable?" said Cairie.

"Of course," said Mr. McGuirk. "I will be returning to Lochgilphead this evening by carriage. In the morn, I will discuss a compensation package, including a transportation allowance, with the regional councilor, and send a telegram to you in Cladich. If it is satisfactory, simply respond, along with a date when you might start. We may want you to work from Cladich until such time as the construction at Campbell House is complete. How does this sound to you?"

Cairie and Jesse were delighted with the good fortune in the opportunity with Campbell House, whose offer Cairie promptly accepted, the first role in some time where Cairie did not have direct supervision of the food preparation. As culinary director for Campbell House she had overall responsibility for the output from the kitchens and knew it would not be a problem to exert indirect control. Colly and Willa were both proud for Cairie and, prouder still, over her manner of serving as Jesse's adoptive mother. They knew, with time, Cairie would become more and more involved at Campbell House as the mother and the daughter adjusted.

Slowly, the years went by. As the commute became regular, Cairie grew more conscious of the inclement weather inherent in a life spent in the western Highlands. Late spring, summer, and early fall were glorious, with long, long days of sunshine and the occasional shower. Sometime in October, shortly after the annual Cladich Fall Fair, things subtlety changed. Mornings were foggy, such as to make it hard to see, slowing down activity; cold, hard rains came from the north and west, off the Irish Sea, and occasionally from the north and east, off the North Sea, bringing chill and mud. Then, in moved the winter's snow and sleet and ice, making travel sloppy and uncomfortable—sometimes the snow flew sideways! Cairie never complained. She had work she loved, and felt appreciated as honors and recognitions were given for her efforts. Rarely, she stayed at the hospital overnight, arranging for Miss Montgomery to spend evenings and nights with Jesse at the Watts Cottage, as it was now known. Not as a chaperone, but more as a comfort and security to Jesse and Cairie.

The more Cairie succeeded at Campbell House, the more Jesse became an independent person. Though normal in the course of events, the idea of Jesse not needing her mother troubled Cairie, however irrational that may be. Jesse had blossomed into a beautiful young woman and had begun thinking of life.

One evening, Jesse said, "Mum, I need to have a life of my own. Not so much separate from you, as with others my own age, for fun and companionship. Surely, you remember what it is like."

In reality, Cairie didn't remember. Economic necessity had led Cairie into a life in the kitchen, beginning when a bit younger than Jesse today. Ma Watts had been supportive, while Cairie's education came in the form of on-the-job training, with long hours and almost no social life. And then she had left for Dumbarton and a long race to the top of her field by her late twenties. She wanted more for Jesse—more than a trade. Cairie wanted Jesse to have a life with diverse friends and, hopefully, to find love when still young enough for a family of her own. If only Garrick were here to help!

And then Cairie said to herself, No! I'll be damned if I am going to let myself put a guilt trip on my late husband because of the unfortunateness of his early death, or anyone else for that matter. Jesse and I will see this through; the two of us will figure it out.

And so, mother and daughter had a talk one Saturday in late winter, with snow on the ground and clouds that threatened sleet at any time. It took two pots of tea and a whole afternoon. They had a talk about the future and specific things: the need to earn a living; getting along in the outside world; sex, love, and the difference between them; thoughts and dreams Jesse had been having; and the unfairness of life, at times. Such a discussion Cairie had never had with her own mother, and for the remainder of her life Cairie remembered how close it made her feel to Jesse. Not surprisingly, Jesse welcomed the talk, had good questions for her mother, and had given thought to life after home. Aware they were well off, even without the assurances from Colly to provide their needs forever, Jesse felt fortunate.

In the late nineteenth century, Scotland and Ireland were going through an exodus due to famine, an economic depression, and a decline in some traditional industries of the region, which gave a large portion of the population of young people not much hope of a good future. Some went to England and Europe; most went to the United States and Canada. To be in a situation with your future secure was a unique position and one to be thankful for. Through a combination of timing, hard work, and an amount of luck, Cairie and Jesse found themselves comfortable in the midst of the turmoil of others. Jesse took this as it came, just good fortune, something to be thankful for and not ashamed of. Cairie realized she had been fortunate, what with her start as a child of a single parent in a thatched cottage, and felt her employment at Campbell House, a quasi-governmental enterprise, as certain a future as could be expected in those times.

Jesse was very popular socially, but her close friends had no hope for a better life and had begun to focus on learning a trade or finding a suitable husband. This put Jesse in a position of not having any peers to engage with as she thought out her future. During a period when Cairie had to spend several nights in Dalmally, Jesse boarded a carriage which took her to the new train station a few miles away, and then mounted a coach for Glasgow, spending a few days with Willa and Colly. She sought out Willa's input on her future, since, as a young woman, Willa had taken care of herself and her ailing father. (Today, we might call Willa's work that of a paralegal, as in those times of sexist diminution, women were prohibited from practicing law, yet could serve as assistants to barristers.) Colly also arranged for Jesse to share a lunch with his old friend Gerald Dickson, the barrister who managed the sale of The Old Speckled Hen for Colly. He had encouraged the romance of Willa and Colly, and was considered almost family to them. Gerald, a busy man, would do almost anything Willa asked, and agreed to talk with Jesse about her prospects.

They met in a conference room at the firm's offices on Queen Street, where a simple, proper lunch had been set. They made pleasant small talk while eating and over coffee and a light dessert. After, Gerald began to probe as to Jesse's interests, intellect, and personality. He found her very well read for a person in their late teens. They discussed a number of the classics. He was shocked to discover she spoke fluent Italian—a talent Cairie had insisted she preserve that linked her life to her birth mother. Gerald was impressed with Jesse's potential and had a delightful discussion with her.

After the lunch, Jesse went shopping with Willa and, as Gerald expected, Colly dropped by the office for some feedback on his discussion with Jesse.

In his normal manner, the Scottish lawyer, brutally honest with Colly, said, "The girl is an exceptional talent. It is a waste to consider her staying in Cladich for her education, as opportunities are too limited. I will speak to my partners tomorrow, and am going to suggest she come to Glasgow and take classes at the University of Glasgow, here in the city. After which, we will have her come to this office and read law with us until such time as she is ready for the barrister's exam. We are a progressive firm and several of our competitors are adding females to the practice of law. I think, with experience, she will be excellent!"

To Colly, Gerald's reaction to Jesse bordered on disbelief.

Gerald added, "Lest you think I am merely trying to curry favor, I assure you I am looking out for the best interests of my firm."

Later that day, Colly took Willa aside while Jesse prepared for dinner, and related his chat with Gerald. Willa was thrilled both for Jesse and for women like her, those denied fair treatment in the workplace. They decided Colly should return with Jesse to Cladich and have a private talk with Cairie, before mentioning anything to Jesse.

After a few more days of shopping and dining, Jesse had similar interviews: with a bank and a lunch with the industrialist Robert Livingston, the same gentleman who had backed Harry Bailey in the purchase of the Hen, from Colly.

At dinner on the final night that Jesse spent with them in Glasgow, they discussed with her how the meetings had gone. She gave a most positive reaction to the luncheon with Gerald Dickson and hoped to see him again as she neared a decision on her chosen path in life.

Colly smiled and said, "Willa has a few things that will keep her occupied over the next few days. If it is okay with you, I might like to ride along on your return to Cladich, see your mother, and get a view of this Campbell House I hear so much about."

"I am delighted for the company," said Jesse. "And Mother will be so happy to see you!"

Colly sent a telegraph that evening so as not to surprise Cairie. The following morning he and Jesse took the train coach and then a carriage on to Cladich. What with the advent of the new train, the journey now took less than a day. Cairie had taken part of the day off, had reserved Colly a room at the Cladich Inn, and insisted on cooking a proper dinner. Colly beamed as he dined with the two McCaig women, before retiring to the inn.

The next day, Jesse went back to school, and Colly accompanied Cairie to Campbell House. Cairie arranged a VIP tour for Colly, after which he returned to Cairie's office. Once there, he closed the door, took a chair, and carefully explained his discussion with Gerald Dickson, regarding Jesse's future. Cairie didn't blink or move a muscle; she just listened while he had his say.

After an uncomfortable period, Colly couldn't stand the silence. "My dear Cairie, are you concerned with my message? I don't want you to think I am acting behind your back. Jesse knows nothing of Gerald's idea," said Colly, wincing at the thought he might have offended her.

With a tear silently sliding down her cheek, Cairie spoke. "Oh no, Colly, I thought nothing of the sort. I am reflecting on the bravery it took for my own mum, Ma Watts, to let me go off on my own all those years ago. It must have crushed her, while she was so encouraging to me. And I must do the same for Jesse."

That evening, over soup and crusts left over from the prior night's meal, Cairie and Colly explained the idea which Gerald Dickson had put forward for Jesse. Colly and Willa had graciously offered Jesse room and board at their place in Glasgow, so she'd have structure and security rather than having to go it alone. And with the new railroad, she could come back to Cladich to visit often or Cairie could come to the city. They knew it was a lot to try and absorb over a short time.

"I want to give it a go," Jesse said, embracing first her mother and then Colly. "I shall miss Cladich and my friends, but I now see a path forward for my life."

There were tears all around. They made more plans, and they thought if Jesse could arrive in Glasgow by late summer, she could enroll in the college for the fall term. And of course they needed to confirm the opportunity with Gerald Dickson. Colly was confident things would come about as planned.

He readied to depart for the city the next morning, excited to tell Willa and to confirm plans with Gerald. Both Cairie and Jesse waved him goodbye as his carriage departed the inn. Then they hugged one another in the knowledge that things were never to be the same.

They spent the next few months preparing for the change. Colly and Willa were handling the arrangements in Glasgow and eagerly anticipating Jesse's arrival. Jesse made a special trip to the city to be introduced to Gerald's partners, where, as expected, her charm and grace sealed the deal. She enrolled in Queen's College for the fall term beginning in September. Jesse's focus shifted from Cladich to Glasgow—time to get on with it. Her mother hosted a party for her school chums as a kind of goodbye. They were happy for Jesse's good fortune and didn't express any jealousies towards her. They were good girls and boys, happy that one in their midst had a chance for greater things than most.

In mid-August, Cairie and Jesse went to Glasgow in order to get Jesse established. They shopped for clothes and schoolbooks, opened her a bank account against protestations from Colly and Willa who wanted to provide for her, and, in general, take care of those things required to establish Jesse in a new place. They thanked Colly and Willa, and Cairie explained she wanted to provide for her only child as any mother would. Jesse needed some privacy or else might feel like a child her whole life. Colly grudgingly understood, while Willa accepted the situation.

And then the time came for Cairie to head back to Cladich and her work at Campbell House. They walked together, the four of them, to the Caledonian train station, Glasgow Central, and waited for Cairie's train to be called. The tension palpable, Colly and Willa sensed this, embraced Cairie and went into a coffee stall, leaving Cairie and Jesse alone. There weren't many tears—this not a time for sadness—rather, it was a recognition of some life-changing event taking place for them both. Cairie had raised Jesse right, mostly by herself, and by all measures had done an amazing job. The realization dawned that Jesse had suddenly transitioned into an adult who needed to take charge of her life and be responsible for any success. Cairie would always be there for her, while the time to step into independence had arrived. They hugged and Cairie boarded the train. Colly and Willa stepped out to join Jesse and they waved goodbye to Cairie as the train left the station.

By pre-agreement, Jesse did not see her mother for several months, not until Christmas, in fact. They expected homesickness to possibly be an issue and the best way to counteract it being a clean break. Telephones were not yet in common use in coastal western Scotland, so the mother and daughter communicated via the Royal Mail. A letter a week from each kept them aware of each other's lives and issues, the weather, Colly and Willa, college studies, Campbell House, the types of things they discussed over the evening dinner table.

Cairie found herself filling the emptiness with more work, additional responsibilities, and less involvement in the happenings in Cladich. Still a good, involved citizen, she left the running of things to others. Cairie had always been a beloved neighbor, and the village felt for her loneliness. She never considered a move to Dalmally; Cladich was her home, and the commute in a carriage gave her time to reflect. She often took dinner home from the kitchen at Campbell House, a way to sample the output while giving herself time to rest. Cairie still tried to get into the Campbell House kitchen from time to time, to keep her cooking skills sharp.

Jesse took well to the city. Colly and Willa gave her space, yet stayed involved in her daily life. The relationship blossomed, which proved good for them all. Jesse loved the college life, young men and women of her station working to grow into another phase of their lives. She studied every weekday evening and on weekends had fun at fairs, dances, art showings, bookstores, and occasionally went to church on Sundays. Her classes were challenging, yet she absorbed knowledge seemingly quicker than her peers. Others sought her out for assistance in learning or dealing with questions about passages of assigned reading. Fall turned to winter, with cold temperatures and snow. With Cairie planning to come to the city for the two weeks over Christmas and the New Year, Colly and Willa were keenly anticipating their "family" getting together again.

Christmas week turned out, in a word, sloppy. The cold and snowy weather required scarves, hats, mittens or a muff, long coats, and boots or galoshes. Even so, people were happy and festive, keen for good times and nostalgia. Though there may have been the occasional scrooge grumbling about the snow and cold, people were mostly pleasant.

Cairie and Jesse walked arm in arm through the falling snow, window shopping, and sharing chestnuts which they bought from a vendor roasting them over a pail of burning coal on the sidewalk. It had been nearly four months apart for them, and they gushed like a pair of schoolgirls while spending an entire afternoon together. Jesse took Cairie to some of her haunts: a coffee shop, a bookstore, and a fancy grocer where Cairie wondered at the vast collection of exotic fruits and nuts, bringing back memories of scouring the wholesale markets in her chef's role. In that age, even for families of some wealth, Christmas wasn't about gifts, but more about food and days spent together, remembrances of times past.

Willa had decorated the flat with some greenery and holly, and scented candles added a touch of pleasantness to the senses, creating a warm and comfortable home.

The four of them caught up with the happenings in their lives, with school going very well for Jesse, and Cairie working too hard, as expected, now with a fair bit of gray in her hair and wrinkles about her ruddy cheeks. Colly and Willa were trying to age gracefully, with time winning; Willa showed a bit of a stoop and Colly's walk had slowed. Life's infirmities were set aside as they celebrated the holiday. Colly hosted them for Christmas dinner at his club: at a table for four, they partook of their own turkey with giblet gravy, roasted potatoes and parsnips, sausages, vegetables and cranberry sauce, and a selection of breads. A very nice bottle of claret accompanied the meal, although they each had a single glass, and Jesse merely took a few sips.

After they had consumed the meal, and before dessert, Colly tinkled his glass and offered a special toast. He said, "Here's to those that I love. Here's to those that love me. And here's to those that love those that I love, and those that love those that love me."

The women gave a light applause, as did diners at several tables nearby, causing Colly to blush.

And then dessert was served: a fantastic Christmas pudding—a concoction of sugar, bread crumbs, suet, raisins, currants, eggs, mixed spice, cinnamon, and nutmeg, boiled in parchment, and then cooled and drizzled with cream and brandy.

Afterwards, they bundled themselves and boarded an open horse carriage for a ride through the Glasgow Green Park as a light snow fell in the gloaming. For the rest of their lives, it remained one of the most pleasant evenings in memory.

In due course, Christmas and New Year were over and routine returned. Cairie took the train back to the coastal Highlands, Jesse returned to classes and schoolwork, and Colly and Willa trudged through the rest of winter. Then the relief of spring, a too brief summer during which Jesse made a trip back to Cladich for a few weeks, and then fall came upon western Scotland. Jesse surprised them with the announcement of her intention to move out on her own before classes started.

"I'm in my twenties now and feel the need for some independence and privacy," she said.

Cairie, Colly, and Willa insisted on paying for her room, board, and expenses. Jesse pointed out that she had substantial funds in the trust Clydesdale Bank had established for her when her father had passed away. Cairie thought of mentioning that she, as trustee, needed to approve of any withdrawals; in fact, Jesse had surpassed the age at which control transferred to her. Best to leave the matter alone; at least Jesse had involved her in the decision. It was a much harder situation for Colly and Willa to swallow; Jesse had not only played a role as granddaughter, she had also served as an emotional and physical support to the aging couple. Jesse assured them she would dine with them frequently and look in on them regularly.

So, Jesse moved into a reconditioned building which offered serviced apartments for female students and the burgeoning number of women professionals in the city. It offered security, a communal dining room, a library, and a laundry service, much like what we think of today as a college condominium complex. The move for Jesse was mostly seamless, and the feeling of not needing to explain every hour or day was liberating. Now she was able to focus more on her studies and friendships, and developing relationships.

At Christmas, Cairie stayed with Jesse and they visited Colly and Willa, a rather awkward change.

One afternoon, with Jesse otherwise engaged, Cairie sat down with Colly and Willa. "We must sacrifice our own emotional needs to give Jesse the freedom and independence she requires at this stage of her life. To do otherwise is selfish," Cairie said.

Colly and Willa looked at each other, nodding. Cairie wiped away tears; she knew what a struggle this had to be for the surrogate parents.

Willa said, "We understand what is right, and we realize now how precious the year we had her."

Colly squeezed his wife and then hugged Cairie. He said, "You know you can trust us to do the right thing."

In early spring, the parties involved felt the time right for Jesse to begin her work and study at Gerald Dickson's law firm. The partners had laid out a plan for roughly two years, during which Jesse focused on the study of law and practical applications of day-to-day legal work. She would be assigned for a period to each of the partners, getting exposure and knowledge regarding specialties. Every three months, the partners reviewed her progress and confirmed the needs of the following period. At the end of the two years, or longer if needed, certainly not shorter, Jesse would immerse herself in an intense study of the technical aspects of the law, after which she could sit for an exam as conducted by the Scottish Legal Society in Edinburgh.

This plan meant long days and serious night study for Jesse. Game and steadfast in her approach, she still made time for a weekly letter to her mother and an evening dinner or weekend lunch with Colly and Willa. However, she significantly curtailed her social life. She understood the long-term benefit of the sacrifice, and sometimes felt completely overwhelmed. This often happened during those gloomy, wet weather periods that plague western Scotland, with rainstorms and gale winds traipsing off the Irish Sea to remind everyone how fickle nature can be. On those evenings, Jesse bundled herself and took an umbrella out into the tempest, letting a wet walk calm her emotions and frustrations. Once appropriately damp and cold, she returned to her lodgings, brewed some tea, and sat by an oil lamp to dry out. By morning, after a restorative sleep, she became her old motivated self again.

During the same period, Cairie struggled with the workload which had somehow come her way at Campbell House. She was so damned efficient and creative, and those in positions of power noticed this and took advantage of her. What had been fun and exciting had turned into work, some not particularly satisfying. Cairie could not learn how to say no when asked to lead some special effort or take another's burden for a time, or work over a weekend, or any number of things which wanted to take over her life. Her ginger hair had quickly gone from slightly gray to mostly white, and she had returned to a demeanor of the old chef days, barking orders and demanding compliance to standards. In short, these were the qualities she had escaped from when she and Garrick took Jesse off to London. Cairie wasn't embarrassed; she wanted to enjoy, rather than endure her remaining lifetime.

She took a week off and went to Glasgow to visit Colly and Willa and to drop in on Jesse. She knew how critical this time had to be for Jesse and didn't want to be a distraction.

The old couple were delighted to see Cairie and happy for her to be their guest for a few days. They now had a cook and housekeeper and went out less and less.

Colly wasted no time in giving an opinion and didn't mince his words. "My dear, your insistence on perfection in every part of your life is simply uncalled for. You act like someone is keeping score or preparing to review what you do," he said. "The days of you needing to prove yourself are years in the past. What is important is what your family and your friends think of you. Your family loves you, and I suspect your number of friends is dwindling, based on your workload!"

Cairie had not expected Colly to be so blunt. Hurt, she had not foreseen judgment or criticism. She wanted sympathy! She couldn't get out any words of response. Colly had given her advice she needed, not what she wanted. It hurt him to disappoint her; he loved her as his own, and anything other than honesty was not something he could abide.

They had something of a constrained dinner together, and Cairie noticed Willa's memory faltering. Cairie realized Colly must be tending to Willa as she passed slowly into the grasp of dementia. He was sacrificing for his beloved wife, and here *she* came, looking for a shoulder to cry on. She felt shame, and then Colly reached over and patted her hand.

"We will be fine, my dear Cairie," he said, "all of us."

Cairie felt relief for the first time in a while.

The next morning, she appeared in the law offices to surprise Jesse, who was thrilled to see her mother. Gerald Dickson uncharacteristically gave Jesse the rest of the day off.

"And take tomorrow also," he said, much to the shock of the staff in the law firm, who smiled at the head partner having feelings.

Cairie mentioned none of her problems to Jesse, nor did she relate the conversation with Colly. They had a light lunch and did some shopping together, simple pleasures in life neither had allowed themselves in a while. They carried in a dinner from a chip house, eating the fish and potatoes with their fingers from the greasy paper wrapper, as Cairie overlooked her culinary discrimination in the interest of a relaxing evening with her child. They talked late into the night.

The next morning Cairie let her daughter sleep, and walked to a local bakery where she bought some scones, clotted cream, and various jams. When Cairie returned, she watched Jesse wash her face. As they ate, Cairie told Jesse about planning to cut back her work at Campbell House. She wanted to take some type of leave of absence of unknown duration and come to Glasgow to assist Colly in the care of Willa.

Jesse demurred, saying, "Mum, I wish you wouldn't. Willa doesn't yet need total care, and Colly is so pleased to be able to help her himself, kind of an act of true love. Maybe if you could arrange to come down a week a month and see how things transition."

That is what Cairie did. When she returned to the coastal Highlands, she met with the regional administrator and laid out a plan to formally begin to delegate responsibilities and otherwise reduce her workload. She planned to spend a week a month caring for an ailing parent and made it clear this was not a request. They knew she had independent means, and, after all, three quarters of a loaf is better than no loaf. Even from afar, the knowledge that Cairie infrequently returned to the North Country kept people at the top of their game.

Over the next year, Cairie took infrequent residence at the flat of Colly and Willa, where she helped in the care of the rapidly declining woman. Colly saw it as a blessing, rather than any type of loss of control.

It was also a blessing to both Jesse and Cairie, who again saw each other more regularly. Jesse, in her final year of clerking at the firm, soon embarked on an intense study in preparation for the Scottish Legal Society examination. Jesse felt a burden for the women in Scotland who hoped for a professional life at that time, near the end of the nineteenth century, what with a now lesser level of gender unfairness which had existed for centuries. She felt her mother had been a sort of pioneer, succeeding in a profession traditionally reserved for men. Were Jesse not to pass the examination, she owned the failure as an indication of women not being as capable. The daughter of Cairie Watts McCaig and failure—never something that honestly entered the equation—Jesse thrived on the pressure. Cairie, and Colly, and Gerald, and others feared the toll it could take. They tried to treat Jesse with kid gloves so as not to add to the stress, with Jesse having none of it.

"If you want to help me, treat me normal, not like some flimsy eggshell!" said Jesse on more than one occasion.

So, the appointed days in Edinburgh came and went. Cairie rode down to the city on the train with Jesse, and they took a room for three nights at the familiar Balmoral Hotel. The exam scheduled for the next morning, Cairie insisted they walk the few blocks to Nyan Fatt Lee's Chinese restaurant. Lee, now aged, still stayed involved in the day-to-day routine. He immediately recognized Cairie and marveled at how Jesse had grown.

"I take care everything," he said. "You two sit here."

Out came the traditional noodles, then fish heads over rice, and green tea. Just wonderful, it went a long way to relaxing a stressed Jesse.

The next morning she hugged her mother goodbye and walked the few blocks under overcast skies, to the building which housed the offices of the Scottish Legal Society. Shown to a conference room, Jesse joined the other candidates sitting for the exam—six men and two women. They maintained complete silence as the questions were passed out by a dour, sharp-faced older clerk. He proceeded to sit on a high stool and watch, as if they were going to try and cheat. Jesse flew through the questions and when the tall clock chimed, she placed her pencil near the sheets of paper, noticing the other two women were also finished, but only one of the men. After a short break, another question was passed out, and so on, until the day ended. The day included no lunch break, although some tea and biscuits were provided at one point. As the day ended, Jesse learned one of the women came from Edinburgh and the other from Aberdeen. No interaction had occurred with the men, as old jealousies die hard. Jesse joined Cairie for a light dinner and then had a restful night's sleep.

The next day was a repeat of the first, with question after question. At the end of the day an officious-looking man came into the room and announced the testing over. The students' sponsors would be advised of their performance.

When Jesse returned to the Balmoral, Cairie surprised her with a special meal at The New Club, hosted by the Operating Committee. Cairie continued to be held in high regard by the Club and they were proud of the progress Jesse had made. Old Leonard, now retired, appeared unexpectedly, breaking into tears when he saw the two women.

The following day, after tea and toast, Cairie and Jesse took the train back to Glasgow, arriving after noon. Colly and Gerald excitedly met their train.

"We've heard, we've heard!" shouted Gerald from the platform.

That morning, the Dickson, Stewart & MacDonald law firm had received a telegram from the Scottish Legal Society. Jesse Adams-McCaig had passed the exam to become a licensed barrister. Colly, red in the face, wildly danced an obscure Scottish jig while waving an umbrella in the air. Cairie worried out loud that he would suffer some kind of attack if he didn't calm down. After hugs around, Gerald related that the woman from Aberdeen and two of the men also had passed.

The group went to the law firm's offices for a celebration held in late afternoon, with tea sandwiches and a large cake. The *Glasgow Herald* had sent a photographer to capture a photo of the new barrister, while a reporter interviewed Jesse and Gerald, all in a whirlwind of excitement.

Colly had arranged for Willa to be there to join in the festivities. Her dementia had visibly worsened and she wasn't sure she knew what to make of the happenings or where they were, but recognized Cairie and Jesse immediately.

Reaching for them both, she softly said, "Proud," while Colly stood alongside and wept with joy.

The next day, Dickson, Stewart & MacDonald offered Jesse a position as a junior barrister, initially focused on Italian banking matters and contracts, and working from the Glasgow office. She asked for, and received, dispensation to return to Cladich with Cairie for a fortnight, to relax and mentally recharge from the long months spent on the intellectual calisthenics necessary to pass the law exam.

Colly gave them a send-off at the train station by himself, because Willa had been overcome by the activities of the previous day and remained home in bed, exhausted.

During the ride, sitting side by side on the train, mother and daughter relaxed and leaned in close, savoring how things were turning out. Cairie had done the best she knew how for Jesse, secure in the knowledge that Paola and Garrick would have approved.

The two weeks spent together in the thatched cottage in Cladich resembled a tonic for them both. They slept late, prepared and ate meals together, and welcomed an almost continuous stream of well-wishers who had learned of Jesse's success. And then Cairie chanced to see a blurb in the regional newspaper publicizing Jesse and her accomplishment. Surely it was the work of Colly, and Cairie felt gratified at the gesture. Cairie took Jesse to Campbell House, where those who had followed her progress over the years greeted her warmly. Proud and quick to point out the adulation belonged to Jesse, Cairie said she had been not much more than a bystander. Those at the hospital had a different opinion, remembering Cairie's sacrifices.

When their holiday ended, the time had arrived to return to normal—or what normal now consisted of. On a damp morning of low clouds rolling off the Irish Sea, Cairie and Jesse rode to Campbell House in a carriage, with the plan for it to take Jesse on to the train station and thence to Glasgow. In Dalmally, they stood by the carriage and embraced, sensing another of life's transitions.

Cairie said, "Expect me to continue to come into the city once or twice a month. I have no doubt you will do your best in the new job, and remember to have a life outside of work. Jesse, I love you and am so proud of you."

Jesse gave her mother a last hug, climbed into the carriage, and went off to live her life. Cairie walked the remaining short distance to Campbell House and thought the lack of rain a good omen. She also needed to get on with her own life, smiling at the thought of focusing, at least a bit, mostly on herself for a change.

Things went on much as before for this group of souls. Cairie managed to continue to reduce her involvement at Campbell House as the rest of the staff rose and filled the void. It wasn't as if the work opportunities at the hospital had fallen out of favor with Cairie; she had taken stock of her situation and felt the need to shift emphasis. She began to spend more time in Glasgow—not a conscious change; rather, she felt needed. Willa had gone into serious decline, and Colly had taken on a nurse for her. Cairie's concerns mostly were for Colly. The stress of the last few years had taken their toll. Always gregarious, Colly had become much more insular, almost withdrawn from his circle of confidants. The strain and worry over Willa was something he internalized, and his old chums found him less pleasant to be around. When Cairie and Jesse were in the picture, his mood improved substantially.

"My day seems brighter when you girls are here," he said to them.

The seasons came and went, tracked not so much by the calendar, as by the weather, gardens, or solar cycle: flowers are here; snow is here; days are long; and days are short. Time waits for no one.

Cairie took a semiretirement from Campbell House, despite the protestations of the staff and administration. The cottage in Cladich became more of a country home, visited in the summer and on holidays. Cairie could afford such a luxury, rare and mostly for the moneyed in those times. Jesse still came to Cladich, yet her visits were more infrequent. The two of them had morphed into city women again. They looked after Colly and Willa and, to a lesser extent, after each other. These were the golden years for Cairie: aging, yet still a comely woman, her hair ginger-gray going white, and complexion perfect. Her time in culinary work had taught her to eat mostly healthily, if not simply. She had a good figure and attracted the attention of more than one potential suitor. Regardless of this, Cairie had been satisfied with the one love of her life, Garrick, and felt her dreams had been fulfilled. She gazed at couples wistfully from time to time, but limited herself to platonic engagements with men from Colly's club or his business relationships.

Colly became more and more reliant on Cairie as Willa's decline became more urgent. In late September, Willa succumbed to pneumonia, the end kind for her.

Not so for Colly, who had trouble accepting her passing. They had married in late middle age and had grown old gracefully together. Since Colly had means, there weren't many things to serve as distractions in their love for each other. They had rarely spent a night apart in the nearly twenty years of their marriage. The first few nights, he felt lost and took to wandering around their flat, wringing his hands.

Cairie arranged for a physician to go to him. "Doctor, he is as the only father I have ever known. I will not have him suffer, nor will I allow him to be medicated into catatonia," said Cairie. "Please help me get him safely through his wife's burial."

The doctor administered some medications to soothe Colly's anxieties. Pharmaceuticals were primitive in those days and care needed to be taken to properly manage doses. With Cairie's help and vigilance, a reasonable medium eventually became established.

Colly and Willa had never had much of a relationship with any particular church. His parents had been staunch Presbyterians and had been close with Pastor Norman, a minister from Dalry who eventually became associated with the Synod office in Glasgow. Cairie called on Garrick's old friend Roddy Hamilton, who had retired from his senior position at the Kirk, Church of Scotland, in Edinburgh. He in turn reached out to Pastor Norman, who agreed to preach Willa Collins's funeral at the United Presbyterian Church of Scotland.

The funeral took place on a Saturday, a typical fall day in Glasgow—that is to say, overcast and gloomy, which fit the mood of the occasion. Cairie sat with Colly in the family pew on the left, the second one in. They were surprised, shocked really, to see Jesse Adams-McCaig arrive for the service, on the arm of a handsome young man. Jesse leaned over and kissed Colly on the cheek, and then they sat in the next pew behind.

For someone who had never met Willa—let alone know her—Pastor Norman did a masterful job of conducting the funeral. He said kind words about Colly's parents and how much membership in the church had meant to them. And he talked of Colly's service to the people of Dalry.

"I've never met a more thoughtful or caring individual than William Colly Collins," Pastor Norman said. "And we gather together today to honor the memory of his loving wife, Willa Cather Collins. May you take comfort in the fact that she passed as she lived, in the arms of both Colly and Christ our Savior."

The burial took place in the graveyard next to the church, a prominent location in Glasgow. A stone had already been placed with Willa's name on it, and Colly's, whose remains would one day rest next to his wife's. When the short service had been completed, the women of the church hosted a simple meal for the family in the basement of the church.

Cairie, almost beside herself to meet the young man with Jesse, sat with Colly at a table to be served salad and a dessert. Jesse started by apologizing to them.

She said, "I am sorry to have brought someone you don't know to dear Willa's service. Mother and Colly, please let me introduce you to Richard McAllister. Richard and I have been seeing each other these last few months, and I wanted him here with me."

Cairie found it awkward, stung by the fact that Jesse had been hiding a beau from her for some time. Still, she set aside her hurt feelings when Richard stood and first shook Cairie's hand and then Colly's.

In a thick Glasgow brogue, Richard said, "Mrs. McCaig and Mr. Collins, it is my pleasure to meet you. Jesse has done nothing but talk about the both of you since we began seeing one another. I have been traveling extensively, which is why we haven't previously been introduced."

Tall and thin, much like Garrick McCaig, he dressed immaculately, down to the perfectly shined shoes, which to Colly's way of thinking, made everything else immaterial.

Anticipating the questions on both their minds, Richard continued. "I am the Scottish representative for Banca Credito Italiano of Genoa. Jesse's firm did some work for us and she is one of a few Scottish lawyers who can both converse and write in Italian. Due to my work, I also speak Italian. It gave us something in common and well, …. You know, sometimes …."—his voice drifted off. "Please accept my sincere apology for being a distraction at this sorrowful time."

"It's my fault," said Jesse. "I insisted he come and give me support. Willa is the only grandmother I have ever known. I …." She blushed profusely as Richard put his arms around her.

Not many times could one catch Cairie and Colly speechless at the same time, but this was one of those occasions.

Pastor Norman broke the spell by walking over to Colly and saying, "Is this the lovely granddaughter I have been hearing about?"

They laughed, and Jesse introduced Richard. The four of them sat and had a pleasant conversation, as families rarely do anymore. As casually as she could, Cairie insisted on making a tea date with Jesse.

The next day Cairie and Colly were due at Dickson, Stewart & MacDonald to go over some financial administrative matters related to Willa's passing. Cairie felt certain Jesse could get free at the end of the day, after Cairie had seen Colly back to his flat. Jesse had recognized the look in her mother's eyes and said she booked them a table for four o'clock at the Queen Street Hotel dining room.

Jesse had already been seated when Cairie arrived. No banter. Cairie said she was disappointed at the idea that Jesse had hidden a romance from her.

"Mother, it somehow happened. I needed to keep it secret until the work had been completed, to avoid the appearance of conflict. Then Gerald asked me to keep it low-key, and one thing led to another. I am truly sorry."

"You mean," Cairie said, "the firm knew, and I didn't. How do you think that makes me look?"

"Mother, be reasonable. People at the firm thought you knew. Everyone felt silence prudent. Now it is out in the open. Please tell me you approve," Jesse pleaded.

Cairie took a sip of her tea, softened, and said to Jesse, "As a daughter, you are too much like me!"

Then Cairie embraced her daughter, and they laughed and began to talk about the future. Richard McAllister had been educated in Scotland, in finance. He had a strong interest in Italian art and Renaissance architecture and chose to do more finance study in Milan. This led him to Banca Credito Italiano and back to Scotland. He was an only child who had been raised in Edinburgh and, first and foremost, a truly nice person.

"I think Dad would have approved of him. I know Colly does," said Jesse.

It was unquestionably a low blow, bringing Garrick into the conversation to bolster her case. However, Cairie took the high road and laughed it off.

The young couple wanted to marry right before Christmas, if, of course, Cairie and Colly approved. Richard, a staunch Presbyterian, hoped to use the same church where the services for Willa had been held. Cairie smiled. She had been looking forward to planning her daughter's wedding, something she dreamed about and made mental notes on for years. Now she barely had three months to take care of everything. Lord, she felt happy.

Richard surprised them both by appearing at the Queen Street Hotel. Cairie gave him a hug and told him she was thrilled for them. She took out some paper and began to make notes. Is the wedding to be formal or informal? Did they have friends to stand up with them? Did they have special music ideas? Should there be a meal after? Sit-down or buffet? What about invited guests? Has a minister been arranged? Where will you live? Cairie was totally frenzied with excitement. How about your parents' role?

At this comment, Jesse recoiled a bit. She had neglected to tell her mother that Richard's parents had both passed on.

Richard said, "It is no problem, dear. She had no way of knowing. I'm depending on her and Colly to be parents enough for us both."

They laughed together, and then the couple rose to leave. Jesse promised to meet with her mother at least twice a week to help plan the matrimonial festivities.

Cairie stopped for some take-away food as she walked back to Colly's flat. She wanted to be sure he maintained a regular diet so as to keep his health stable. She told Colly about the plans of Jesse and Richard, and he clapped his hands in joy. Maybe this could be something which brought some luster back into his life. Cairie knew for sure it did for her.

The weeks went by quickly and suddenly early December arrived with cold and frequent snow. Shop windows were decorated for the Christmas season, and people were in a better frame of mind. Cairie and Colly were invited to the holiday party for the Dickson, Stewart & MacDonald law firm. They were seated at the partners' table, a special honor which they appreciated. Jesse and Richard were at the event also, of course.

The wedding barely a week away, the tension built. Colly had insisted on paying for a formal wedding dress for Jesse, handmade by the finest dressmaker in Glasgow. He also had a mother of the bride dress commissioned, and the women's final fittings were together. They laughed and giggled and squealed like schoolgirls, much to Colly's delight.

Jesse had moved out of her serviced apartment and into Colly's place with him and her mother. The flat became wedding central, with Colly smart enough to stay out of the way. As these things go, the situation remained calm. Cairie's planning skills, combined with Colly's contacts and Jesse's calm demeanor, meant assured success.

The day of the wedding, the sky looked like snow at any moment. At midmorning, a horse carriage took them—Jesse and Cairie and Colly—over to the church with Pastor Norman there to perform the service. Guests were beginning to arrive, and Cairie had a few, last private moments with her daughter in a room off the narthex. Jesse beamed absolutely radiant, and Cairie looked as proud as could be.

She whispered, "I love you," into Jesse's ear.

Then an usher led her down the aisle to the second pew on the left, the family's pew. She slid into the pew and sat next to Colly, just the two of them. Though he had tears flowing from his eyes, his tremendous joy for Jesse and Richard, and Cairie, muted over Willa not being there to enjoy the marriage of their adopted granddaughter.

The organ music began, and they stood as the procession entered the church. Jesse and Richard walked up the aisle together, arm in arm, followed by a select group of friends who were members of the wedding party. Pastor Norman thanked everyone for coming. Then he asked who gave this woman into matrimony.

By pre-agreement, Cairie stood and calmly said, "Her father, Garrick, and I do."

Pastor Norman continued with the formal vows between the two young people. It seemed like a blur to Cairie: Ma Watts, Cairie's leaving Cladich the first time, the years of toil in the many kitchens, finding love and losing it, mothering Jesse, the return to Cladich and Campbell House, Colly and Willa, and the move to Glasgow. And now this. Life had come a complete circle.

Cairie sat, weeping silent tears of joy in the second pew as the pastor pronounced Richard and Jesse, husband and wife. The young couple turned and faced those in attendance, blushing and smiling, filled with hope and promise.

At the same moment, the sun slid from behind a cloud, causing a brilliant whiteness to shine on the far, snow-covered hills of the Scottish countryside.

Life goes on. It always does.

# Acknowledgments

The author wishes to thank story consultants Mindy Lynch Lytle and Mary Ann Evans Pierce for their support and encouragement, and is grateful to Robert Sellery, whose prodding led to the completion and publication of the trilogy. Beth Mansbridge provided the professional copyediting.

# About the Author

William Lynch is a writer of fiction and nonfiction. A native of rural Indiana with deep Scottish roots, he has traced his family history to the late 1700s, when they fled Ireland for Scotland in search of work.

In real life, his travels enabled him to visit Scotland more than thirty times, occasionally to the countryside southwest of Glasgow where his ancestors toiled in the shaft mines for coal.

Writing the quasi family memoir novella *The Life and Times of Jackie Brodie* rekindled his fascination with the culture, history, and pride of those hardy individuals who lived, loved, and died in western Scotland in the late 1800s.

This new collection of novellas is a celebration of those people and times.